**'Were you ever hit? Shot, I mean?'
The question was quiet, and filled
with a lot of other questions.**

'No.' Logan straightened and looked
directly at Karina. 'No.'

That wasn't a lie. A dead hostage was no
use to anyone. The guns had been pointed a
metre either side of him, the bullets kicking
up the dust close enough that he'd felt the
grit on his legs, the warning explicit. *Don't
think you can get away.*

Logan looked deep into Karina's eyes, saw
nothing but her big-hearted concern and felt
his heart roll. His finger touched her chin,
his thumb slipping over her smooth skin.

'But you had a bad time?'

'Yeah, Karina, I did.'

Then he bent and brushed his lips over hers
to stop her talking any more. Except the
instant his mouth touched hers he had to
have more, had to lose himself in her. His
arms came up and wrapped around her,
hauling her warm, soft body in close against
his chilled, frightened one. He could forget
the horror while Karina deflected him.
He deepened his kiss. Karina returned it,
meeting each of his moves with one of her
own. Then her arms slid around his neck
and pulled him even closer and he felt safe.
Warm and cared about and *safe.*

Dear Reader,

Many years ago I moved from Auckland to the small rural town of Motueka—talk about a culture shock! But once I got my head around no traffic lights, and all the apples and kiwifruit anyone could wish for growing everywhere, I quickly discovered some of the most wonderful people and made a lifelong friend there.

When I wanted to tip Karina Brown out of her usual Auckland haunts and into somewhere that could nurture her I naturally chose Motueka, and let the locals work their magic on her, too. And then along comes Logan Pascale—and if ever there's a man who needs help it's him. Of course it's Karina who really gets him back on his feet, with her big heart and a ton of love to share.

I hope you enjoy following these two on their journey to happiness.

Cheers!

Sue MacKay

THE FAMILY SHE NEEDS

BY
SUE MacKAY

First published in Great Britain 2015
by Mills & Boon, an imprint of Harlequin (UK) Limited,
Large Print edition 2015
Eton House, 18-24 Paradise Road,
Richmond, Surrey, TW9 1SR

© 2015 Sue MacKay

ISBN: 978-0-263-25502-7

Printed and bound in Great Britain
by CPI Antony Rowe, Chippenham, Wiltshire

With a background of working in medical laboratories, and a love of the romance genre, it is no surprise that **Sue MacKay** writes Mills & Boon® Medical Romance™ stories. An avid reader all her life, she wrote her first story at age eight—about a prince, of course. She lives with her own hero in the beautiful Marlborough Sounds, at the top of New Zealand's South Island, where she indulges her passions for the outdoors, the sea and cycling.

Books by Sue MacKay

A Family This Christmas
The Midwife's Son
A Father for Her Baby
From Duty to Daddy
The Gift of a Child
You, Me and a Family
Christmas with Dr Delicious
Every Boy's Dream Dad
The Dangers of Dating Your Boss
Surgeon in a Wedding Dress

**Visit the author profile page
at millsandboon.co.uk for more titles**

To Jacqui.

Thank you for the keys to your house,
a sympathetic ear, lots of advice I mostly
ignored, and the best ever parties. It might've
been a long time ago but I've never forgotten.

Praise for Sue MacKay

CHAPTER ONE

'I'M AFRAID IT'S a no from this bank, Miss Brown.' The manager stood abruptly, indicating the interview was over.

Karina gritted her teeth to hold back a sharp retort. Miss Brown? In a town where everyone from millionaires to bag ladies was on first-name terms, she had just been insulted. She'd lived in Motueka for a little under a year but no one called her *Miss* anything. She was Karina Brown. End of. Had been since the day she'd left Auckland in a blaze of flashing media cameras and pushy reporters shoving microphones in her face as they demanded answers to questions she'd had no intention of answering. The day she'd gone back to her maiden name and left her old life behind to go and reinvent herself.

'Thank you for your time, Mr Pederson.' She gave the same back through clamped jaws.

Rising from the chair, she was astonished to

feel her legs shaking. Smoothing down her knee-length pencil skirt and tugging her shoulders back tight inside her tailored jacket—not worn since Auckland—Karina strode out of the bank manager's office with all the aplomb of her old persona. She would *not* grovel for the money she desperately needed to buy the other half of the house—not yet. Being told no just increased her determination to achieve her goal.

'How'd that go?' Rebecca called, only loudly enough for her to hear.

Crossing to her friend, who was more commonly known as Becca, despite her name badge, stationed at the bank's customer service desk, Karina shook her head. 'A big fail. Apparently I'm not a good prospect for lending money to.'

Ironic, considering her background. Once upon a time several hundred thousand dollars had been chickenfeed to her. Nowadays she lived on the wages she earned as a nurse at the medical centre she jointly owned in the small rural town of Motueka, far removed from that glamorous life. She had a tiny nest egg, put aside for rainy days, but nothing big enough to buy out Logan Pascale.

'Don't you dare think like that,' growled Becca.

'I showed him the property valuation and suggested I could spread the loan out for thirty years.' She'd be sixty-four and nearly ready to retire by then, but it would be worth it.

Becca leaned closer. 'It shouldn't mean a thing, but half the problem is you're not a local. Here, coming from the Big Smoke up north is like coming from another country.'

'I've heard that enough to know it's true.' But it didn't explain the malicious gleam in Pederson's eyes as he'd told her no. He'd been enjoying himself at her expense. 'Bet he's looked me up online.'

'Are you sure you want a mortgage hanging over your head? Couldn't you ask someone in your family for the money this once?'

'What?' Karina shuddered. Prove to her father that what he believed had been right all along? That she couldn't make it on her own? 'No!' she barked, too loudly.

Becca wouldn't understand her need to stand on her own two tiny feet and do what was right for a little boy who relied entirely on her for everything.

'I can't do that,' she reiterated, more quietly. This was the toughest test she'd faced so far in her stand to be independent. *So suck it up and beat the odds.*

'I figured that'd be your answer, but don't let your pride get in the way of what's right.'

Jeepers, Becca, be blunt, why don't you?

'Anything I do will be what's right for Mickey.'

Mickey. The boy she loved as if he were her own. As one of his two guardians, she intended doing everything within her power to make sure she kept the only home he'd known. She'd promised his parents no less.

'How *is* that bundle of mischief? I haven't seen him for days.'

'Mickey's cool.'

Damn, but this was hard. She also needed to keep everything exactly as it was for herself. She'd crafted a new life in which she was in control and happy, in a quiet, comfortable way.

'Just the usual hiccups. Not enough honey on his toast and me putting the wrong shirt out for him to wear to kindergarten.'

'I bet you give him everything he wants.'

'How can I refuse when he gives me that gappy grin? But this morning he was very clingy and didn't want to go to kindergarten. Most unusual. Said his tummy was sore.'

'Did you insist on him going?'

Karina shrugged. 'Jonty's looking after him while I'm here.'

Becca returned to the original problem. 'What are you going to do about buying out Dr Pascale now?'

'Know a millionaire with lots of cash stashed under his bed?' A few hundred thousand was all she needed but, hey, in for an apple, in for a sack full of dollars.

'You want a sexy hunk to go with those millions?'

'Rich *and* sexy? All in one package? What's the catch?' Because she'd had that package and knew the pitfalls all too well.

'I don't know any guy around here fitting the description.' Becca grinned.

'Just as well.' Karina smiled back, thankful that her friend hadn't pointed out which of them actually knew the most millionaires.

'You still don't want to put your toe in the dating pond?'

'That's the last thing I want. I'm enjoying being

in charge of my own life. Why would I want to give that up to be told which functions to attend and who to invite to dinner?'

Becca chose not to answer that. Instead she went with 'Heard when the good doctor's actually arriving?' A gleam of excitement lit up her eyes.

'Not a dickey bird. I don't even know if he's left Africa yet.' Hopefully he was still out in the wilderness, working with people who needed his medical skills. 'The longer I hear nothing, the longer I've got to come up with a solution for the house.'

But the days were running out—fast.

'Wonder what he's like? Even if he doesn't have millions under his bed he could be sexy.'

'Like *that's* going to make a difference to anything.'

The situation was complicated enough, with them sharing guardianship of Mickey and having joint ownership of the house and attached medical centre. They'd never met, which suited her perfectly. She'd kept everything ticking over since Maria and James had died. Dr Pascale hadn't made it home for his brother and his sister-in-law's funeral—hadn't talked to Karina at all, even by phone. Their only communication had been through the lawyers acting for the unusual partnership put in place solely to protect Mickey.

When a letter had arrived from the estate lawyers stating that Dr Logan Pascale wanted to sell the property and invest the money for Mickey's future, she'd felt a familiar punch in her stomach. Only this time she refused to fold. This time she would stand up to anything being thrown at her and would not be told what to do. Mickey shouldn't be moved away from all his memories of his parents.

When Maria and James had approached her about becoming a guardian if the unthinkable happened, she'd promised to do everything to make Mickey happy. Maria, her best friend ever, had hugged her and said that was exactly why they were asking. Now she had a promise to keep.

Putting that aside, Karina said, 'Guess I'd better be getting home.' She turned to stare out through the glass doors and shivered at the sight. 'It wasn't raining when I walked up here.' Though the sky had been grey and threatening. 'My car needs two new tyres.' It sat in the driveway going nowhere in the meantime.

'I'd offer you my truck, but my brother's borrowed it.' Becca handed her a large umbrella with bright blue logos splashed across it. She winked. 'Compliments of the bank. They're only for our most important clients.'

Karina couldn't speak for the sudden lump in her throat. *Thank you*, she thought as she stared at this woman who'd unexpectedly become a good friend. *Thank you*. Hopefully Becca understood.

The wind blew rain into her face as she headed down High Street towards home. Home, Mickey, the surgery: her life. The life she liked to think she controlled.

'Mostly…' she muttered as the rain got worse.

Within minutes her skirt was soaked and her blouse was getting damp down the front. Her jacket hadn't been designed to be closed across her breasts. Very classy, but totally impractical for her newer, more prosaic lifestyle. She hurried along the footpath, quickly giving up on avoiding the puddles. She'd have jogged all the way, but given she was wearing three-inch narrow heels—all to impress an unimpressionable goat of a banker—she figured that might be a little crazy even for her.

The cooler air did nothing to chill her anger at being refused a loan. She should have asked on what grounds she'd been turned down, but giving Mr Pederson the pleasure of knowing he'd upset her hadn't been an option. Now she'd have to think of another way to raise the capital. *Oh, yeah, like how?* Short of selling herself down at the wharf, there weren't any ideas shining out at her.

Shoving the disappointment and her sense of unfairness down deep, where she kept insurmountable problems, she focused on reaching home as soon as possible. Before lunch she needed to change Jonty's wound from when he'd fallen in the chook pen and caught his forearm on a stake.

Dear old Grumpy Jones. Secretly, she adored Jonty. Underneath all that griping he was such a sweetheart, and so helpful. Without him she'd never have got the garden dug in time to plant spuds and onions. He'd complained about it with every turn of the soil, but when she'd tried to wrest the spade from him he'd given her an earful.

A gust of wind slammed into her and caught the umbrella, turning it inside out. The heavens poured water onto her carefully styled hair and turned her blouse see-through. So much for trying to look half-decent for once. Of *course* the bank's umbrella was rubbish. Went with the miserable manager's image.

Locking the gate at the bottom of her driveway, she turned for the house and groaned. The hole in the asphalt had overflowed, sending water streaming out to the road. Water, water everywhere…

'It's so tempting.'

Despite her angst with the world she felt a flicker of mischief unfurl deep inside, and she raised a grin. Might as well get some fun out of the day and act like the delinquent Mr Pederson believed her to be. This hopelessness needed stomping on—and stuff the shoes. It was doubtful she'd be wearing them again anyway.

Karina breathed deep and leapt into the air to land in the shallow hole. Splashes of murky water shot in every direction, including up her legs. Up, down, splash, splash. She pretended the tears leaking from the corners of her eyes were from pure pleasure, and not exasperation at her inability to fix the current crisis.

'I want to do that!' Mickey yelled from the veranda.

'Come on, then.'

So the sore tummy had recovered. She watched anxiously as he leapt off the steps and charged towards her.

'Go easy,' she muttered. She hated that he believed he was invulnerable. But she also acknowledged that his condition mustn't hold him back.

Splash. Mickey's round face split wide into a grin. Bending his knees, he bombed his feet into the deepest water he could find. His shrieks filled the air, and soon Karina was laughing hard. To hell with banks and money and everything. *This* was what life was about: enjoying the little things, and especially having fun with this boy she loved so much.

When Mickey was totally soaked she grabbed his hand and started for the house. 'Let's get into dry clothes and then I'll make us hot chocolate drinks.'

'Can we?' Mickey shouted. *'Really?'*

'I reckon.' She bounded up the steps and kicked off her shoes. 'Is Mr Grumpy here or out in the shed?'

'Inside our place.'

She untied Mickey's laces and tugged his shoes

and socks off. 'Straight to the bathroom, please. Get out of those clothes while I find you some dry ones.'

'What about my hot chocolate?'

'After you've changed.'

She ruffled his hair and gently pushed him inside, before banging the door shut behind them. Dropping her sopping bag and the useless umbrella into the bucket in the corner, she spun around to head to her bedroom and pulled up short at the sight of a man walking towards her.

'Who are you?' she gasped, though from the way goosebumps were lifting her skin she already had an inkling. So much for hoping he was weeks away. But, hey, it was that kind of day.

'Logan Pascale.' The long and lean, tanned man held a hand out to her. 'You're Karina Brown?' His eyes were very wide, and definitely not focused on her face.

Automatically putting her hand in his, she tried to lock eyes with him, but he was staring at something below her chin. When she followed the direction of his gaze she gasped again. Every last scrap of her clothing was wet, clinging to her like plastic wrap, and her blouse was more see-through than if she'd worn nothing. Her breasts pushed hard against her bra…her very lacy, transparent bra.

Open up, floor, right now. Gobble me up.

When nothing happened she dredged deep for what little pride she could muster. 'Yes, I'm Karina.' She lifted her head to study the stranger who held the future of Mickey's home in the warm, strong hand she was still holding. Snatching her hand free, she stepped back and returned to scrutinising him.

'Jonty let me in. He's popped home for a moment.'

Despite the chill settling over her due to all that wetness, warmth eased through her body, touching her tummy, her toes, her face. He might be too lean for her taste, but her body didn't seem to care if the way it responded when she looked at him was an indicator. His face was gaunt, as if he needed feeding up. But those eyes were what really caught at her. Piercing, yet guarded, while also holding a hint of humour and compassion. A disturbing mix.

Oh, man, this was so *wrong*. The guy should come with a warning label. *Don't come near un-*

less you hold all the aces. She was short on aces today. Worse, she couldn't stop staring.

Tall… Okay, anyone was tall compared to her. Oh, and he had the most gorgeous crop of over-long black hair, while his day-old stubble made her mouth water.

'Karina, I want my clothes!' Mickey yelled.

'Coming,' she called back, far more quietly.

'I'll wait for you in the kitchen,' her distracting visitor told her. 'Want me to make that hot chocolate I heard you mention?'

'With marshmallows, ta.'

He was already acting as if he lived here. She shrugged. *Get over it*. Logan Pascale owned half the place; he could come and go as he pleased. Was that good or bad? That warmth he'd engendered evaporated, leaving her shivering with cold and apprehension as she opened drawers to find Mickey some clothes.

Logan did hold all the aces. He wanted to sell the place she'd made her home and had believed she'd live in for many years to come. He had as much right to make decisions about the property and Mickey's future as she did. But had he even heard of joint decisions? Her sigh was filled with annoyance and frustration of the most irritating kind. If he thought selling up would help his nephew's cause then he didn't know damn all about Mickey.

But of course he didn't. Visiting briefly once a year meant he hardly knew his nephew. Hadn't seen the day-to-day growing up stuff, didn't know what he liked and hated, wouldn't understand how the Down syndrome affected him.

No doubt Logan intended getting things done fast so he could fly away again, leaving her to cope with the mess he'd created.

Well, think again, Pascale. I'm made of stronger stuff. You won't get away with it. I've grown a backbone because of men like you. Men who charm women out of their three-inch-high shoes all because they have a hidden agenda.

CHAPTER TWO

LOGAN DRAGGED HIS eyes forward and headed to the kitchen. His mouth twisted into a tight smile. He might have stopped staring at that bundle of unbridled energy, but her image still seared his brain. Her small body, with those clothes moulded to each and every curve, those enormous eyes the colour of the hot drinks he was about to make blinking out of that elfin face.

From the little he knew about her he understood that she'd walked away from an extremely comfortable life and all that entailed. He certainly hadn't been expecting to be surprised by her energy for life. When he'd first seen Karina carrying on in the driveway, before Mickey had joined her, he'd thought she was a teenager playing hooky from school, not the qualified nurse taking care of his nephew.

He'd felt a delicious shock when he'd realised those curves certainly didn't belong to a teenager, but instead to an all-grown-up woman. A very tempting grown-up woman. It wasn't difficult to imagine running his hands over that body. *Damn it.* He couldn't afford to get sidetracked, even for a few hours. He might have been living the life of a monk lately, but that would have to continue at least while he visited Motueka and sorted out Mickey's future—starting with making arrangements to sell this place.

'Kar—ina, where are you? I'm ready.'

Did Mickey ever talk in fewer decibels than a jet on take-off?

'Coming, kiddo.'

At least Karina replied quietly, in a soft, almost caressing tone.

Caressing. As in stroking, touching…

Logan stomped through to the kitchen, where everything appeared spotless. Nothing like what he was used to in the over-used, under-tidied kitchens of Nigeria, where all energy went into helping people rather than putting things away in cupboards only so that someone could remove them again moments later. This was kind of a nice change. Homey.

Whoa. They were going to sell this place. Getting comfortable and cosy wasn't an option.

He had no difficulty finding chocolate to go into the milk he'd put on to heat. A stack of bars stood right beside the tin of drinking chocolate powder in the pantry, along with packets of marshmallows. He popped a marshmallow in his mouth as he stirred the milk, savouring the sweet burst of flavour on his tongue.

Karina bounced into the small space, using up what little air there was, bumping him with her elbows or hips every time she moved—which was constantly. While those curves were now hidden under trousers and a chambray shirt, he knew they were there. Her hair was damp and curls were beginning to fly, adding to that waif-like appearance.

'Will you look at that?' She nodded in the direction of the window. 'It's already stopped raining. Put on for my benefit, was it?' She came closer and peered into the pot. 'Looking good. Pour Mickey's before it gets too hot. He doesn't like waiting for it to cool.'

Trying to ignore the scent of roses and damp hair wafting around her, Logan reached for the mug she held out. 'Sure. He's grown heaps since I was last here.' *Concentrate on Mickey and the perfume will eventually evaporate.* He hoped.

'Kids do tend to grow and change quite a bit in a year.' She placed two more mugs on the bench. 'I presume you're joining us in our hot chocolate moment?'

'Might as well.'

There hadn't been a hint of sting in her words, and yet the guilt they caused tightened his gut enough to ache. He hadn't been the best uncle, or brother, over the years. He knew that more than anyone.

'I would've been back nearly two months ago except for an exceptional circumstance.'

Why justify himself to this woman? It was none of her business. Except…

'I'm sorry you've had to shoulder all the responsibility for Mickey since James and Maria died.' Not to mention the medical centre that had been James's pride and joy, and had seemed too dull to *him*.

She shrugged. 'No worries.'

'Understatement your thing, is it?'

This house had had more than its share of problems due to lack of maintenance over the years. The lawyers had made sure he knew about every last fault. At least that was something he could, and would, fix. He had an appointment at two o'clock to talk to a real estate agent and get the property on the market. Getting it up to scratch was part of his agenda over the next few weeks.

'Not that I'm aware.' Karina opened a tin from the pantry and placed some cookies on a plate. 'I'm sorry you missed the funeral. We held off as long as possible, but no one could track you down.'

Wow, she had a way of ramping up the guilt without even trying. His gut wanted to regurgitate that marshmallow.

'There are often days—weeks in the rainy season—when all contact with the outside world is lost.' He wasn't going to mention that, where he'd been at that critical time, contact with anyone had been impossible.

A small hand rested on his forearm, orange-tipped fingers splaying lightly on his shirtsleeve. Each fingertip was a heat source, tripping through his chilled body and reminding him of easier times. Carefree times.

She said quietly, 'I wasn't having a poke at you. I understand the difficulties. James mentioned how hard it could be to get hold of you in Nigeria.'

If only the reason had been that simple. His eyes locked with hers, saw nothing but genuine sympathy there. Sympathy that should be tightening his shoulders and making him prove he didn't need it but was instead undermining his determination to remain aloof and do what was needed as quickly as possible before he headed back to a world he understood.

But he didn't understand it. Not any more. Strange how the easy look in Karina's eyes made him long for a break, here, in this quiet town where people really were safe. To be able to take each day slowly, get his body back in shape, his head thinking straight, and to get to know his nephew. Time even to get to know Karina Brown.

Jerking his arm away, he snapped, 'If it had been at all possible to get here I would've.' He drew in a deep breath, tried for calm. 'But it wasn't possible.'

If he'd stepped one foot outside his prison hut

his body would have been riddled with bullets and he'd have been left to the flies and the vultures.

Hot milk splashed on the bench as he poured the liquid into the mugs.

Karina deftly wiped up the spill before dropping two marshmallows on top of each drink. 'Mickey, sit up at the table. You can have one cookie before lunch.'

She perched on a chair beside the boy, holding her mug in both hands, her gaze thoughtful. Was she trying to believe he'd been telling the truth?

'How did you get on at the bank?' he asked, in an attempt to distract her from his apparent failings as an uncle.

'How did you know that's where I was?' She shifted on her chair, began twisting the mug back and forth between her hands.

'Jonty mentioned it when I introduced myself.'

'That surprises me.' She sighed, then stood up abruptly. 'I'd better go see if I'm needed before surgery closes for lunch. Keep an eye on Mickey, will you?'

Oh, no, you don't.

Logan cut off her mad dash by taking her arm

and holding on until she turned to look up at him. 'I've been over there. Everything's under control.'

'You checked up on my surgery?'

Could those eyes get any bigger? 'Isn't it *our* surgery?' he asked quietly. 'I wasn't checking up on anything. I was introducing myself.'

The air hissed over her bottom lip as she sagged in on herself. Pulling her arm away, she dropped onto the chair she'd hurriedly vacated.

'Yes, I went to the bank. No, they won't lend me the money I need to buy you out. Any further questions?' she snapped.

He lifted out another chair, flicked it around to straddle it, and folded his arms over the top. 'Why do you want to buy me out? Doesn't it make sense to sell this rambling old place, with its huge grounds, and buy a new, comfortable, easily kept home?'

'No. It. Doesn't.'

The words fell like heavy weights between them.

'This is Mickey's home, the place where he remembers his mum and dad. I will *not* take him away from here. He gets upset enough as it is some days.'

'I see.'

'Do you?' Those perfectly shaped eyebrows lifted. 'What about the surgery? If we sell the house, where's that going to be relocated?'

'I'd have thought that'd be the last thing you'd want to be bothered with. I know you struggle to keep a GP full-time.'

She could have told him what he already knew, that she'd managed with locums so far. But she didn't. Instead she went for his throat. 'Unless you have plans to take over?'

Logan stood up so fast the chair knocked against the table. 'Are you out of your mind?'

Him? Working in a small town, dealing with the everyday stuff of colds and stomach bugs and high blood pressure? Signing on for ever?

'That would not work. Believe me.'

He strode over to stare out of the window onto the drive, with its hole that needed repairing, and swore silently. Not in a million years. He wanted to be with people who had no choices, who were forever grateful for any little help they got. People who came and went so quickly they didn't cling to his life.

Mickey banged his empty mug on the table. 'I want to play with Mr Grumpy.'

Karina didn't move, almost as though she hadn't heard Mickey. Even if the neighbours probably had.

Logan turned. 'Who's Mr Grumpy?'

'He teaches me things.' Mickey slid off the chair and picked up his mug to bang it on the bench. 'Doesn't he, Karina?'

'Yes, he does, sweetheart.' She stood up. 'And I should've changed Jonty's dressing before now.'

Definitely looking for an excuse to escape him.

'Can it wait a few more minutes and I'll come with you?' When she looked at him with astonishment, he hastened to add, 'I take it Jonty and Mr Grumpy are one and the same.'

Karina's lips twitched. And sent his hormones into a little spasm. She really was seriously distracting.

She told him, 'Yes.' And then, turning to Mickey, said, 'Mr Grumpy should be in the potting shed, planting the tomato seeds. If he's not you come straight back here and we'll find him together. Okay?' She held her hand up, palm out.

Mickey high-fived it. 'Okey-dokey, hokey-pokey.'

Logan watched his nephew racing from the room and felt his heart stir just a tiny bit. Having Down syndrome wasn't holding the kid back from enjoying himself.

'Does he understand fully what happened to his parents?'

Sadness filled Karina's eyes. 'As much as a kid his age can. Sometimes he asks when Daddy's coming home from work, or if Mummy's going to make his dinner. There are nights when I find him crying into his pillow. But then I've found him doing that when he's lost his favourite toy, so I could be completely wrong and he hasn't got a clue why he now lives with me.'

'From what my parents told me, you had a lot to do with him before the accident.'

Not a stranger, like him. Guilt raised its head again. Mickey hadn't remembered him this morning. No surprise, considering he'd been about three the last time Logan had flown in for a quick visit. Thank goodness James had had the good sense to make Karina joint guardian with him. Even if she wasn't family in any DNA kind of way, the boy had a firm constant in his life and wasn't coping with a man who preferred working and living in exotic places. Make that who had *used to* prefer.

Mickey needed security—he needed the same people in his life day in and day out, to see the same kids at playgroup every time he went. He certainly wouldn't get that tagging along with his uncle to desolate places on the African continent. Besides, that wasn't an option after what had happened on his last tour. Far too dangerous.

Karina spoke quietly. 'I'd been working here for a few months when the accident happened.' She blinked furiously. 'Mickey and I were great mates even then.'

'Coming from Auckland to such a small place must've taken some getting used to.'

'It was refreshing.' She picked at a spot on the table. 'Maria and I met in Auckland while doing our nursing training and became firm friends. Inseparable at times.'

She raised those beautiful eyes to his face and the sadness spilling out made him want to wrap her up in his arms and hold her tight.

He didn't. Because he mightn't be able to let her go. Because he needed to be held, too. Because he should have been here for Mickey, and even for Karina.

'You were Maria's bridesmaid. I vaguely recall a wedding photo.'

'Hardly a bridesmaid when those two went out to lunch and came back married. They dragged me along, saying they had a surprise.'

'There was a guy there as well.'

'The law requires two witnesses.'

The words were flat. Her face had gone blank, her eyes expressionless.

The devil got hold of his tongue. 'Who was he? I didn't recognise him as one of James's friends.'

He'd recently gone weeks without talking to anyone, bar demanding to be freed, and since then he'd apparently lost the ability to be circumspect.

'My ex-husband.'

Never had he heard so much emotion in two little words. Anger, disappointment, despair, hurt, and a whole lot more. Something beyond his shoulder seemed to fascinate her for a long, drawn-out moment. Then she blinked.

'We split very suddenly and I wanted a change of environment. Staying on in Auckland no longer worked for me.' She continued spilling her guts.

'About that time Maria decided to be a stay-at-home mum and asked me to fill her place at the surgery. I think she made that up, because she'd been managing very nicely until then. But I arrived here within days and I'm not likely to leave again.'

'Only now you've got a wee boy.'

And a big heart. She didn't appear to be struggling with everything she did, and yet her days had to be close to chaotic at times—especially given that Mickey needed a lot of attention with his condition.

'A boy I'd do anything for.'

He got the message loud and clear. *Don't mess with Karina. Or Mickey.*

'So what do you do for a social life in Motueka?' Might as well ask anything that came into his brain while he had her talking.

Karina shrugged. 'Friday night drinks at a bar on High Street with a friend is more than enough for me. As I've no intention of marrying again I'm not joining the dating circuit.'

Unbelievably honest.

'I can understand that.'

Way too much information, Logan. He knew

from the slight widening of her eyes that she'd read between the lines of his simple statement and understood he was as uninterested in finding a soul mate as she was. He'd seen far too many relationships bite the dust in Africa. Commitment to the health organisation left little time for anyone or anything else.

Karina said, 'You want to sell this place?'

She was forthright. He'd give her that.

'Yes.'

He'd be the same.

'Why?'

'I've seen the builder's report the lawyers have had done. This place needs major repairs and maintenance, which won't come cheap—especially for a property nearly eighty years old. A comfortable house with no financial worries for you seems a good idea. Though what you'd do for jumping puddles I'm not sure,' he added, forcing a smile.

A smile that she chose to ignore as she stood up, stretching as tall as possible on her toes, which still left her well short of his chin. 'Haven't you left something out?'

'Like what?'

Those eyes that had entranced him now appeared to be ready to slice him to shreds. He was about to get an earful. Her cheeks were reddening, her mouth tightening.

'The bit where you will then be free to fly off into the sunset, knowing there's nothing here for you to worry yourself over. Your nephew will be well cared for, and he won't miss out on a thing because there won't be any repairs to pay for. You'll have done your bit for your family.'

His family? Yes, she certainly knew how to twist the knife. As he opened his mouth to explain that his nephew was better off being with her, she cut him off and added to his distress.

'I will never sign any sale agreement you draw up. *Never.* Get it?'

Her forefinger stabbed his chest—hard. Strange how he wanted to wrap his hand around that finger and kiss the tip.

She hadn't finished. 'This is Mickey's home until the day he doesn't need one any more.'

She couldn't have put it more bluntly than that. Yet he sensed a well of emotion and need behind her statement. What for, or why, he had yet to figure out. He'd also have to work harder on persuading her that his way was best for all of them. And the reasons she believed were not necessarily behind his thinking. Though she wasn't entirely wrong about those either.

CHAPTER THREE

OF ALL THE stubborn, thoughtless, selfish men in the world, Logan Pascale had to be top of the pile. Karina bit down on the words threatening to spill off her tongue and headed out to the shed to find Jonty. The stubborn, thoughtless, selfish man followed her.

'I need to replace that dressing for you,' she informed the older man down on his knees trying to unscrew the broken handle of a spade. She'd do her best to ignore Logan for now.

'They don't make these handles like they used to,' Jonty grunted.

Beside the old man Mickey sat on his butt in spilled potting mix. 'I'm helping Mr Grumpy.' He reverently held a pair of pliers in his hands.

Jonty didn't look up as he said, 'I don't need the dressing changed. There's nothing wrong with this one.'

The bolt suddenly flicked free and spun across the floor.

Mickey crawled after it. 'I got it.'

Karina squatted beside Jonty. 'You don't want to get an infection.'

'Pish. I'm healthy. No infection's coming near me.' The second bolt was giving him as much trouble as the first.

Logan hunkered down on his haunches opposite them. 'How'd this break?'

Go away and leave us be. Her teeth snapped shut, sending vibrations through her skull.

'Damned rocks,' Jonty griped.

Karina wasn't giving in. 'Let me see that arm, please.'

The old man glanced at Logan. 'Women, eh? Bossy creatures—think they know best.'

Logan laughed: a warm sound that briefly lifted her black mood.

Then he won points by saying to Jonty, 'I know what you mean, but in this instance I think Karina's right. An infection in your arm could be debilitating for some time. You might have to delay finishing that digging.'

Jonty's knuckles were white as he tried to budge the bolt. 'I guess.'

'Here. Can I get that?' Logan asked in an off-hand manner that made it easy for Jonty to accept his offer.

'You do that while Miss Bossy, here, does her nurse routine.'

Smothering a smile, Karina removed the dressing and cleaned Jonty's wound. It would have been better doing it inside, but Jonty would never agree. 'It's looking good. You were very lucky not to have that spike go any deeper.'

'I got two dozen eggs this morning,' he muttered.

Good, there'd be some spare to trade for fresh bread at the bakehouse down the road. 'They're laying well, considering it's winter.'

'There you go.' Logan handed back the screwdriver and a few screws.

'You look like your brother.' Mr Grumpy squeezed Logan's shoulder. 'Sorry about James, lad. We miss him and Maria around here.'

Weren't men supposed to be reticent? Mr Grumpy had said more words in the last ten minutes than he often uttered in a whole day.

Karina taped on the new dressing and gathered up the old one. 'There you go.'

'Thanks, lass.'

'Is Mickey okay with you until I've got lunch ready?'

Jonty rolled his eyes and took the spade minus its handle back from Logan.

'That's a yes, then.'

She thought Logan would remain in the shed, but he was quickly on his feet to go with her.

The problem with walking towards the house after having heard Logan mention maintenance was that she looked hard at the weatherboard walls and window frames. The paint was peeling in places, and some of the boards did show signs of rot. The putty around the glass panes had cracked and in places had fallen out completely.

'Yeah, it does need an overhaul,' she admitted grudgingly under her breath.

The guy had supersensitive hearing. 'A major undertaking, involving a lot of time and effort to restore the whole building.'

She spun around, skidding on the sodden grass. His hand quickly caught her arm, steadied her, then instantly dropped away.

Rubbing the place where those strong fingers had gripped, she raised her head and told him, 'Think about how wonderful this old building could look with a new coat of paint and those windows picked out in a shade of green to fit in with the grounds.'

The large grounds in which the lawns were mowed once a month, whether they needed it or not, summer and winter. And in which the trees should have been pruned and the wayward hedge needed cutting off at the roots.

Logan's eyebrows were in danger of disappearing under that mop of dark hair. His flat mouth quirked up into an annoying smile. 'You have a wonderful imagination.'

'What are your plans? Are you in town for long?'

'As long as it takes to make you see reason and get this place on the market.'

He didn't half labour the point. The breath she dragged in chilled her bottom teeth. 'Then you'll be here a long time.'

Could she ask him to leave his half of the money in the property as a loan to her? No, she couldn't.

She'd only just met him, but she was over his in-
credulous glances already.

'I'll buy a lotto ticket tomorrow.'

'Why not go easy on yourself and accept that
selling is the right thing to do?'

Logan held open the back door and indicated
she should go ahead of him. Heading directly to
the bathroom, she dropped the small bag contain-
ing Jonty's old dressing into the bin. Her head
spun with retorts but she managed to keep the
brakes on her tongue. He didn't—and wouldn't—
have a clue how important a refuge this house was
to her. Here, she was in charge and her opinion
counted. Here, her family and her ex didn't tell
her what to do with her days.

Back in the kitchen, she got out the bread and
margarine, some hardboiled eggs and lettuce, and
began making sandwiches. The clock didn't stop
for Logan. She needed to get back to work.

When he parked his butt on the corner of the
table, looking as if he had no intention of moving
until he got his point across, she knew a moment
of fear. What if he won this crazy battle and the
house was sold out from under her? Would it be
so bad to live in another house in Motueka? *Yes,*

it would. Jonty wouldn't be next door, griping and grumbling at her while he watered her vegetables, or complaining that he hated boiled carrots more than tinned peas and yet eating every last mouthful on his plate whenever she cooked his dinner—which was most nights else he'd starve. He'd never learned to cook; his late wife had been old-school and believed that was her role.

Another argument against Logan's plan to sell was that the medical centre would have to shift. Or, worse, close down, forcing the patients she'd come to know to transfer to other centres.

Surreptitiously studying this stranger as she spread margarine, it shocked her to realise that he looked as though he belonged here. He had every right to be here. No denying that, much as she wanted to. But looking as if he fitted right in—that was too much to absorb. So she wouldn't. She'd carry on the fight in the hope that eventually she'd get it through his very handsome skull that she meant every word she uttered.

Starting with: 'You honestly think I should walk away from this?' She waved her hand in the direction of the surgery through the wall. 'Tell all the patients, "Sorry, but we're not interested in looking out for you any more"? People don't like change, Logan.'

'Are you sure it's not you that dislikes change?'

This man went straight for the heart of the matter every time.

She pretended she hadn't heard him. 'Especially the older folk. They know their doctor and nurse, and they trust them to know their backgrounds without having to delve into files for an answer about who their son is or where their grandchildren live. That sort of thing distresses them.'

'Except the current locum's only been here three months and plans on leaving within the next three. Where's the continuity in *that*?'

He didn't miss a trick, which sucked big-time.

'I won't change my mind.' Her voice was rising and she didn't care. This man riled her.

'I'm getting the picture.' He folded his arms over his chest, the movement diverting her gaze from his inscrutable face to those muscles that underscored the polo-necked jersey he wore.

'So am I,' she muttered, not quite sure whether she was referring to his stubbornness or his mouth-watering chest.

Either of them was a problem. Logan was nothing like his brother in physical shape or appearance. James had been of average height and had carried a bit more weight than was healthy. But he'd had an open face and oodles of kindness and generosity. She wasn't sure where Logan was with those characteristics.

'Where are you staying while you're in Motueka?'

'Here. That's if you don't kick me out on the street. I like the spare room at the back of the house.'

Wanting to say no to that idea didn't mean she could.

'There's no space to swing a cat in there.' It was tiny and filled with cartons that needed to be gone through. 'It's also an ice box, being so far from the fire in the lounge and the heat pump in the hall.'

But she knew nothing about this man.

'It will suit me perfectly.'

'What's wrong with the room next to Mickey's? It's bigger and warmer.'

Why make him comfortable? If he didn't like the room he might leave earlier than planned.

'I figure I'll be out of your hair down there.' His eyes zeroed in on the sandwich she was making.

Avoiding eye contact? 'I noticed all the cartons. I'll shift them into the other bedroom after lunch.'

'They're full of James and Maria's personal belongings. I haven't had the gumption to go through them. Anyway, I thought you should be the one to deal with James's stuff.'

And I'll keep putting off sorting through Maria's until finally I can do it without instantly bursting into tears. If only I could throw everything away untouched.

'I probably should.' Logan sounded equally reluctant to tackle that issue. Which she couldn't fault.

'I'll try to get around to it before I head away again.'

Since Logan seemed intent on steamrollering her opposition to selling they'd be at loggerheads the whole time and he'd probably be glad to leave sooner rather than later. Behind her back she crossed her fingers.

'The wardrobe's locked. It's the only way to keep the door from bursting open and spilling files and books across the room.' She tried one last time. 'You sure you don't want the other room?'

Those smoky grey eyes roamed the kitchen before returning to her. 'The small one's fine. Better than some places I've been lately.' He sucked a quick breath on that.

'I'll find some linen.'

'Karina, I don't expect you to run around after me. I'll make my own bed.'

'What *do* you expect of me, then?'

'To seriously consider my proposal to sell. In fact, you might as well come with me to see the real estate salesperson.'

'I what?' The knife slid out of her fingers and clattered onto the floor. 'Haven't you listened to anything I've said?'

'Have you listened to *me*?' he asked, in a cool, calm tone.

What would rattle this man? Except for those moments when his eyes had looked everywhere except at her he'd remained in control, no matter what she'd said. Which was warning enough. She knew controlled and controlling men better than most.

'I've heard every single crazy idea you've come up with so far!' she yelled.

Get a grip. This is not the way to deal with him. Think about Mickey. That's it. Sweet little man

*that he is, he needs you to bat for him, but sensi-
bly, not like a shrew.*

She tried to rein in her anger. 'Maybe it would
be better if you stayed in the motel down the road.'
It didn't come out quite as calmly as she'd hoped,
but it was an improvement.

Logan remained perched on the edge of the
table, totally unperturbed at her outburst. 'I want
to have as much time as possible with Mickey before I head away again.'

She pounced. 'And when might that be?' Now
she was repeating herself.

'Probably not as soon as you'd like.'

Did his lips twitch? She'd swear they had, which
was kind of deflating . If she wanted to be treated
fairly then she had to do likewise.

'I'm making one rule. We don't talk about selling while you're staying in this house.'

'Karina, apart from seeing Mickey and sorting
out some legal stuff with the lawyers over James
and Maria's wills, the only purpose of my visit
is to sell. See it from my point of view. I can't do
a thing to help you around the house when I'm
overseas. If you're living in a new home I won't
have to worry about that.'

'I see.'

He sounded too darned reasonable. Didn't mean she was prepared to change her mind, though. Was she being selfish? Not at all. For her, this wasn't about repairs and maintenance—it was about having a home. Not a house; a home. She'd had houses, mansions, and she knew how cold and impersonal they could be. She'd come to Motueka to turn around her life and find out what she really wanted for herself, and she had created a little world right here that would suit her for years to come. The thought that Logan wanted to take that away frightened her.

'I don't want you worrying about me. I'm not your concern. Only Mickey is.'

'The way I see it, if you're happy then so is my nephew.'

'Then you've nothing to worry about. I'm happy living right here.'

Her tummy tightened. *Huh? It's true. I am. Aren't I? I was until this morning. And I will be again, the moment Logan understands he's wrong about this.*

'And if you're really worried about the medical centre and the house, why don't you move here permanently? You could share in making Mickey happy. He'd love to have you around the place.'

Logan didn't bat an eyelid, didn't have a fit as he had earlier when she'd suggested the same thing. 'Give me some time to catch up on what happened with James, and get to know Mickey properly, and I'll postpone that appointment with the agent.'

'You're bribing me now?' She found a small smile for him. 'Stay one month and I'll listen to you at the end of that. I'm not saying I'll go along with your plans, but we'll discuss them then.'

And I'll spend that whole month showing you why you're wrong. I'll also be busy finding the funds to buy you out.

'Fine.'

Another twitch of those lips. Had he read her mind as easily as that?

Leaning back against the bench, Karina fought the need to study him while he stared at his feet. The expression on his lean face was sad and worried, as if he didn't know where to go with any of this after all. *Well, blow me over, rover. This guy has some serious issues.*

Folding her arms under her breasts, she tried to deny the compassion building up for him. She couldn't let it rule her head. Instead she needed to focus on what was best for Mickey. And then for her.

One thing was for sure: Logan Pascale would not be good for her. At all. Yes, but he would be great for one little boy who struggled to understand why his mum and dad didn't walk in through the door at the end of the day as they'd used to.

Logan wanted to laugh, which was a surprise in itself. Karina was as transparent as clear water. He knew he was going to be hounded over the coming weeks. He should go and book into a motel immediately. But he'd play the game. He'd only been in this house a couple of hours and already he didn't want to leave. The building was old and draughty, the windows rattled when the wind gusted, there was a bucket in the laundry, catching drips, and the carpets were threadbare. But, as Karina had said, it was a home—not just a house with two people rattling around in the vast spaces.

'Lunch is ready.' Karina pushed a plate laden with sandwiches across the bench towards him.

'Want me to get Mickey?'

She nodded. 'And Jonty.'

'Why am I not surprised?'

Filling the kettle, she shook her head at him, those curls flying around her face and causing his gut to clench.

'He looks after my gardens and hens and I give him some meals. Green dollars.'

'Yeah, sure. Nothing to do with a kind heart or friendship?' He couldn't resist winking as he stood up, ready to stride out of the kitchen.

What a woman. Too darned diverting for his own good. Mickey and his eager smiles had already caught at him, so throw in Karina with her exuberant, even fiery spirit and he was knocked off his feet. He hadn't experienced anything so normal in a long time. He didn't want to now.

In Africa he knew his role—understood that there were no long-term connections with his patients, the women he worked with, the places he lived and worked in. He was there simply to help people less fortunate than him who needed his medical skills. Plain and simple.

Apparently others had thought he could also provide a source of money for their militant operations. Their illegal activities. The militants had got the wrong end of things when they'd kidnapped him, believing he was the son of a wealthy English lord. That lucky guy had been whisked away to safety the moment the CEO of the African Health Organisation had realised what was going on.

No wonder this place felt like a slice of heaven with its everyday normality.

Logan knew he was being a pain in the proverbial by choosing a room that Karina obviously preferred him not to have, but it suited him perfectly. He might have explained that after sharing cramped quarters with his colleagues for as long as he had he relished the idea of having space to himself. What he wouldn't tell her was that he had to have privacy at night.

Sweat popped on his brow. Karina was right in that he should find a motel, only not for the reasons she'd been espousing. One night here and she'd be kicking him out anyway. Not to mention the awkward questions she'd be asking if he had his usual problems.

He focused on the mundane, hoping the other, darker thoughts bothering him would fade for a while.

Instead of going to get Mickey to come for lunch, he said, 'I was under the impression Mickey went to kindergarten all day?'

'He usually does, but a sore tummy kept him at home this morning.' Karina lifted one shoulder. 'After that puddle-jumping I'd say he's fit to go this afternoon.'

'Want me to drop him off?'

'Sure.'

'What time do you finish work?' he asked when he returned with Mickey and Jonty in tow.

'Five-thirty, give or take.'

'Then you come home to cook dinner?'

Karina nodded and smiled. That smile pushed the darkness inside him further back.

'I hope you're happy with risotto?'

'Sounds good to me.'

'Mickey usually gets dropped off at the surgery about four. If you want to spend time with him you can collect him then.'

Her smile expanded, sending a flood of heat right down to the tips of his toes, heating all parts of his body on the way.

'He'd love that. You're family, Uncle Logan.'

His head dipped up and down in agreement as

he swallowed the crazy need for her she'd inadvertently cranked up all too easily even while she'd been so ruthless in her comments about what he wanted to do to her haven. Again, Karina hadn't held back on pressuring him, but he was getting used to her forthrightness. If he used it wisely it could save them both a lot of the trouble that ducking and diving around their problems would cause.

'Mickey mightn't understand, but I'm right beside him all the way.' His mouth lifted into a small smile. A rare occurrence recently. 'But you have a point. I'm not used to small boys.'

'I'd have thought many of your patients would be small boys. Boys of any size and age, really.'

'I used to kick a football around in the dust with plenty of young lads, but somehow getting to know Mickey seems daunting.'

Terrifying, even. There wouldn't be any second chances. He had to get everything right from the get-go. There was a lot riding on that—things like Mickey living a happy childhood despite losing his parents.

Karina laughed, and it was as though the sun were in the room with them. Her face had that cheeky, fun quality she did so well. That wild hair was a riot of curls now that it had dried. What would it feel like to run his fingers through those coils? To feel them spring against the palms of his hands?

'Right,' she said. 'That's you sorted. Unless you'd prefer Mickey gives kindergarten a miss and stays with you?'

'What do four-year-olds like to do with their afternoons?' Damn, he hadn't meant to say that out loud.

'Believe me, Mickey will order you around and run you ragged.'

Did she have to look so pleased?

Unfortunately Karina's smug look had turned out to be justified. Logan grimaced as he sidestepped another spray of muddy water Mickey sent his way. What was it with small boys and puddles? The rain might have stopped hours ago, but the water swamping the lawns hadn't drained away and didn't look as if it would any time soon. Another problem that needed looking into. Like that hole in the driveway, which definitely had to be sorted.

'I want to see Karina.' Mickey stood before him, staring up with those eyes that reminded him so much of James.

James. His older brother. Logan's heart squeezed tight. They hadn't been close, but they'd always known the other was there if needed. Hence the guardianship thing. He'd been touched when James had asked him, yet he'd thought he should have asked Mum and Dad. Apparently they'd believed Mickey needed younger guardians. They also hadn't been comfortable at the prospect of living on remote Stewart Island with Mickey.

If he ever needed urgent medical attention, getting off the island wasn't as simple as getting on board a boat and starting the engine. Weather ruled down there. It was a place his parents had fallen in love with, and they'd moved there the moment he'd finished school. It wasn't a place he'd ever thought of as home.

Logan sure as hell hadn't expected to take up the role of guardian so soon, if ever. It was only supposed to be insurance—the kind you took out but never used. If he'd known what would happen only weeks later he'd have told James to find someone better suited. Not that his brother would have listened.

A small hand wrapped around his fingers. 'Karina's at work.'

'Yeah, buddy, I know. So we'll have to wait to see her.'

Mickey shook his head. 'No. I want to see her now. I need to go pee-pee.'

'I'll take you inside.'

Mickey's head turned from side to side. 'No. Got to go to work.' He began tugging at Logan's hand. 'Come on.'

A cheerful-looking man glanced up from the counter as they walked in the front door of the medical centre. 'Hi, Mickey. Sounds like you've been having fun.' Then his gaze swooped to Logan. 'You must be Logan. I'm David Maxwell, the current locum. Sorry I missed you earlier.'

'Hey, good to meet you. I never had any intention of dragging you from your patients when I dropped by. I was just eyeing the set-up.' Logan held out his hand. 'This little guy wants the bathroom. Apparently you've got a better one than what's at home.'

David chuckled. 'What we've got is Karina.'

So Mickey and Karina had bonded completely. That was good for the little fellow. He was very lovable. Even after a few hours Logan knew leaving him again wouldn't be as easy as he'd expected.

'How does he cope when he's at kindergarten?'

Karina answered from another room. 'There are good days and there are not-so-good ones. His teacher's quite strict, but sometimes I go and get him and then he sits in here with me and his colouring-in book.'

'I need pee-pee, Karina!' the subject of their conversation yelled.

In the waiting area people laughed.

David grinned. 'You'd better hurry, Karina. It's looking a bit urgent out here.'

She appeared in an instant. 'Come on, Mickey.' Then over her shoulder she muttered to Logan in a very cheeky tone, 'Think you dodged a bullet?'

He shuddered. Karina's bullets would be comparatively harmless compared to the real thing. 'Apparently you're a dab hand at this.'

'You'll keep.' She flapped a hand at him before following Mickey down the hall.

'Keep?' David asked in a hopeful tone. 'You're

not looking to hang around permanently, by any chance?'

Hating to disappoint another person already, he shrugged, but finally had to be honest. 'No, my contract's still running with the organisation I work for.'

'Motueka isn't just a quiet town in the back of beyond. There's always lots going on.'

That hope was fading.

'After the places I've been, it's fair heaving. If I ever did come back permanently I think I'd prefer living and working in a place like this. Big cities don't hold any attraction for me.'

If he ever came back? Why would he? What was here for him?

A little boy who had yet to call him Uncle? A boy who needed a man in his life?

A feminine laugh floated down the hall from the direction in which Karina had disappeared. Okay, there might be another attraction, but he couldn't change his life plan for a woman.

'Life plan? More of a total stuff-up.'

'Sorry?'

He'd forgotten David was still standing there,

looking hopeful and resigned all at once. 'Talking to myself. Not a good look.'

'I guess you've got a lot to sort out at the moment, without me dumping the surgery problems on your shoulders. We can have a chat in a few days.' Then he looked worried. 'You will be here for a while, right?'

'Right.'

Exactly how long was 'a while'? This was another round of questions he wasn't dealing with very well. Harmless enquiries and yet they ratcheted up the tightness in his arm muscles, in his chest.

Glancing around, he saw people in the office, the waiting room, the hall: all innocent of anything but normality. Normality he struggled to fit into. By the toy box in the waiting room a toddler lunged for a wooden truck and shrieked at the top of his lungs.

Logan knew that the ear-piercing, gut-tearing sound came from the little boy. Knew it. But somewhere in his head he was hearing one of his fellow hostages as she was beaten, screaming her fear and rage and pain.

That same fear, rage and pain thumped at his temples.

Suddenly he was so tired he could barely stay upright. Exhaustion gripped him, drained his body of every drop of energy. Exhaustion that sleep would not fix. Only exercise might.

It was happening again. He couldn't blame jet lag. That might be compounding the debilitated state he found himself in, but it wasn't the cause. That remained back in Africa. In the form of dangerous men armed with machine guns and the inability to listen to reason. Men who thought the quickest way to riches was holding innocent people to ransom.

'Are you all right?'

David was staring at him with that same wary look he'd seen in his colleagues' eyes all too often since he'd been freed.

'I'm fine.' His voice rasped with tension. 'I need some fresh air. Tell Karina I've gone for a walk, will you?'

Tell her I'm sorry I'm leaving Mickey with her while she has to work. Tell her I apologise for coming here before I'd managed to quash the demons lurking in my skull.

He ran for the door.

CHAPTER FOUR

KARINA ROLLED OVER in bed and held her breath. Something had woken her. But what? The house creaks as usual, but otherwise everything seemed quiet. She must have been imagining things. Punching her pillow into shape, she curled up on her side and closed her eyes.

There it was again. A low moan—followed by a cry.

Slipping out from under the warm bedcovers, she shoved her feet into slippers and pushed her arms into her thick robe. Out in the hallway she listened for a minute but heard nothing. Had Mickey called out? Carefully opening his door, she checked him over but he was sound asleep.

Karina returned to her room as a cry cut through the quiet, lifting the hairs on her neck. It came from further down the hall. Logan? Had he fallen and hurt himself?

Outside his door, she hesitated. If the noise

hadn't come from in there, she'd look a right idiot, bursting in and waking him. Leaning her ear to the door, she heard mutterings from the other side. It sounded as though the man talked in his sleep. She smiled. Who knew what she might learn if she felt inclined to listen in? Straightening up, she began to turn away. There was still that noise to check out.

'Don't touch me, you pig!' Logan shouted.

At least she presumed it was Logan, even though his voice was pitched higher than usual and filled with hate. Was that fear in those words? It sounded as if he needed help. What if someone else was in the room, attacking him?

Flinging the door wide, she flicked the light on and stared around the room. Nobody but Logan. He lay sprawled across the bed, the sheets wound around his legs, his arms thrashing against the mattress at either side of his hips. His skin glistened with sweat, and yet he was shivering. His eyes were wide, staring at the ceiling, then at her, then cruising the walls. Back to her. Not seeing her or seeing anything. As though he didn't know where he was.

'Who are you? Get out of my hut.'

Oh, my God, he's having a nightmare.

Wary of those flailing arms, she reached to touch his shoulder. 'Logan. Wake up. Logan. You're having a bad dream.'

She shook him gently. His arm swung up and out. Karina stepped back, felt his fist graze her thigh. This time she snatched at his arm, held it tight against her body, shook him as gently as possible.

'Logan. Wake up. It's Karina. You're in Motueka. You are safe.'

Was this the right thing to do? Should she be trying to bring him round more slowly? But how?

'Did you say Karina?' Logan blinked at her. Then looked around the room, tried to peer past her. 'Where did you say I am?'

'You're at James's home. Remember? Where Mickey lives.'

In her tight grip his arm began relaxing, the tension slowly ebbing away as reality dawned in those gunmetal-grey eyes.

He said nothing, continued to stare at her, not quite believing her.

'Motueka. Mickey, Karina.' She enunciated

slowly, clearly, hoping the significance of those words would reach him.

Did this have anything to do with his sudden mood change that afternoon? David had told her Logan had become agitated and taken off for a fast walk. When she'd asked him about it later he'd fobbed her off with some nonsense about needing fresh air. As if the air in the back yard where he'd been playing with Mickey had been stale and old?

Lowering his arm to his side, she spoke quietly, so as not to disturb him unduly. 'Logan, I'm going to cover you with the quilt. It's freezing in here and you've got goosebumps on your arms.'

He also had scars on his chest and his ribs were too close to the surface. Not enough muscle or fat covered him. As if he'd been ill. What had the nightmare been about? Was it linked to the state of his body? What would he do if she gave in to the need to hug him to her? To kiss away that pain darkening his eyes to the colour of cold slate? If she ran her fingertips over those purple lines on his skin, would he yell at her?

Carefully keeping an eye on him, in case he hadn't completely returned to wakefulness, she retrieved the quilt from the floor and covered him right up to his chin. 'There you go. I'll flick the electric blanket on for a bit. It'll warm you faster.'

Logan wanted to curl up and die—or at least to hide under that quilt so Karina never saw his face again. He'd just blown everything. She'd never leave Mickey with him now. Not even for five minutes. She'd think he was a veritable nutcase, and she'd be right.

But hiding was pointless. She'd seen too much already. Next the questions would start. Why? When? How often did these nightmares occur? Questions he'd never answer. The shrink had told him they were part of the process and to accept them—to talk about them, even. Eventually they'd stop.

Eventually couldn't come soon enough. He was adamant he wouldn't talk about them. Especially not to Karina.

Slowly he raised his eyes to her face and saw nothing but concern glittering out at him. Concern for him? He did not want that, so he went on the attack and grabbed her hand. 'Did I yell out?'

She nodded. 'A couple of times.' Bending down,

she fluffed around at the side of the bed until he heard the switch for the blanket click on. 'Don't worry about it. I always sleep with one ear open, listening for Mickey.'

'You didn't need to come into my room. I'm not exactly a child.'

He was upsetting her, but how else to divert those questions that must be burning her up?

Her usually open countenance shut down, and her concern was withdrawn as her face tightened. 'I came in here because I thought maybe you'd fallen and needed help. That's all.'

'Can you turn the light off?' He dropped her hand as quickly as he'd caught it.

'Sure.'

The dark held all kinds of terrors but he needed to hide his eyes from her all-seeing gaze. Thankfully even with the light off the room was still partially lit from the hallway. Perfect, really. Half-light kept the demons at bay and saved what was left of his pride.

Karina asked from the doorway, 'Want a cup of tea?'

'No. Thanks.'

'I'm going to make one for myself.'

'Karina—' His tongue flicked across his lips. 'I apologise for any inconvenience.' He looked at the wall on the other side of the room. 'I don't know what happened.'

Lying didn't come easy, but what else was he supposed to do?

He wasn't fooling her at all. He'd bet his debatable sanity that she knew this wasn't the first nightmare he'd had. His recovery from this episode screamed *Been there, done that—often.*

Her smile returned, as it always did. If he'd learned anything about Karina since arriving it was that she smiled a lot. Except when she talked about her ex-husband.

'Sure you don't want a drink of some sort? Hot chocolate?'

Karina's voice penetrated his topsy-turvy mind, helped bring him further back to the here and now of the pokey room that was temporarily his bedroom until he could persuade this woman to sell.

'Treating me like one of Mickey's playmates now, are you?' The smile he gave was as false as most elderly people's teeth, but acting normally was beyond him at the moment. When she didn't answer, he said, forcing more lightness into his voice, 'Hot chocolate would be good. Three marshmallows this time.'

'Be back in a few minutes. Don't fall asleep while you're waiting.'

'That's not going to happen any time soon,' he muttered.

Experience told him he'd lie awake for hours, fighting sleep and the evil that waited there for him. Those scumbags had a lot to answer for.

The moment he was alone he hauled his aching body out of bed and pulled on jeans and a sweatshirt. He was cold, yes, but more than that he'd seen Karina's eyes slide across his chest. He'd seen her assessing the way his ribs poked out, seen her gaze stutter on those raw scars crisscrossing his torso. He did not need reminding of how he looked after weeks of surviving on one plate of gruel a day. He knew. He did not need to see the scars to remember the pain of being slapped with a machete. It had been weeks since he'd studied his body in a mirror. It would be months before he looked again.

God, his legs were wobbly. He sank back onto the bed, felt the warmth seeping up from the electric blanket. Luxury. A simple thing and yet he began to thaw, in his muscles and around his heart. *Thank you, Karina.* Maybe his wariness of people might take a backward step in this crazy, mixed-up home where genuine kindness was the order of the day.

Karina heard Logan poking at the fire in the lounge and took his chocolate drink and her mug of tea in there, careful not to switch on the main light as she entered. As much as the chocolate tempted her with its sweet smell she had to be kind to her hips occasionally.

'Here you go.' Placing the mug on top of the firebox, she turned to head back to bed. There were a million questions buzzing around her skull but she knew better than to voice them.

'Stay while you drink your tea...'

The hesitancy in Logan's voice spoke to her in a way his usual in-control tone could not have.

'Sure.' Sliding into one of the two armchairs placed at either side of the firebox, she leaned back and propped her feet on the wood basket. It was kind of cosy with the half-light and the quietness of the house. She loved night-time. The dark had always been her friend—like a child's comfort blanket. In the dark she made the most sense of all her problems.

Logan blew on his drink. 'I'll move to the motel tomorrow.'

He sat on the edge of the other chair, leaning his elbows on his knees, the mug held between both hands. The sweatshirt he'd pulled on might cover the chest that had drawn her attention all too easily, but even covered and in the semi-dark the view wasn't half bad.

'Stay here, Logan. The motel's proprietors won't make you hot chocolate at one in the morning.'

He chose not to answer. Did that mean he agreed but hated to admit it? If so, then he was telling her the nightmare would reoccur.

'So...' She sipped her tea and looked to lighten the tension that was turning his knuckles white. 'Tomorrow being Wednesday, Mickey has gym time at three-thirty. Want to take him?'

'I guess I'll have mastered the pee-pee trick by then.'

'There's no trick. But you might have to be firm about not bringing him to me. He's taken to you quite quickly, but I'm still the main constant in his life. Anything new makes him seek me out.'

His smile was wan, but at least he tried. 'Is he likely to cause a scene if I insist on taking him to the bathroom?'

'Possibly. I can be there if you want. I take an hour off on Wednesday afternoons.'

'How do you do it? You don't appear to be asleep on your feet, yet you should be. You make me tired thinking about everything you manage to fit into your day. Did Mickey always go to kindergarten full-time?'

The questions were coming thick and fast—possibly in an attempt to distract himself from that nightmare.

She explained how things worked around here. 'It used to be mornings only, but now he's older and I'm working full-time, he goes all day. He loves socialising with other kids, and he has a best friend, William.'

'You said something about listening out for Mickey during the night. Does he wake a lot?'

'He's getting better. At first, after James and Maria died, he'd wake three and four times. Now it's barely that often in a week.'

Logan chewed his marshmallows and blew on his drink. 'I haven't had this since I was a kid.'

'It's one of those comfort drinks, isn't it?'

'Yes.'

Oh, cripes. He'd be thinking she was treating him the same way she did Mickey, when he had his waking moments. 'I didn't mean—'

'I like comfort drinks.'

'Good.'

What else could she say? Did he like comfort hugs? Sexy hugs?

Wash your mouth out, Karina Brown.

Why? She'd love nothing more than to feel those strong arms wrapped around her, holding her against that chest. Even looking out of condition, his chest tempted her—sad puppy that she was. It had been a long time since a man had held her because he cared about her.

Yeah, and if Logan did hold you, what then? You'd stand there pretending you weren't horny as hell? Because you would be. Parts of your body you'd forgotten existed are already heating up with desire.

No, she wouldn't have the strength to step back and pretend she could take or leave his hug. It would be impossible not to give in to the unusual sensations that had been assaulting her from the moment she'd first set eyes on him.

Logan asked, 'How do you feel about being a full-time caregiver to Mickey? It can't have been easy, stepping up when you were single and not used to parenthood.'

Right. So he wasn't thinking of anything hot and sexy.

Giving herself a mental shake, she answered the question and ignored the other part of what he'd said. 'There wasn't time to think about it. I got the phone call about the accident and went immediately to collect Mickey from the babysitter they'd left him with that night. From that moment on I've been his mum. And dad. Surrogate, maybe, but there's no one else.'

He needed a real father on hand. A male role model. Preferably a permanent one who didn't disappear to the other side of the world for a year at a time.

'Your parents have visited twice, staying a few days. They're great with him.' And with her. Adele and Mark Pascale never made her feel uncomfortable about raising their grandson, instead encouraging her with everything.

'How did you feel when Maria and James asked you to be a guardian? Did you realise what it would entail?' Logan spoke softly, as if aware that he might be stepping outside the boundaries of where their relationship allowed him to go.

She could ask him the same question. The only difference being that he was family while she wasn't. It was a bit strange.

'At first I was shocked. Then I felt honoured. But, hey, I never expected I'd actually be stepping up to do it.' Even now, the fact that Maria and James had asked warmed her, especially on the days when she doubted her ability to do a good job. 'As to your other question—yes, I was fully aware of what looking after Mickey meant.' Another gulp of tea. 'I have never regretted signing those papers. Not once.'

'I didn't mean to suggest you might have. I apologise if you got the wrong idea.' Logan looked uncomfortable.

'Were you comparing my reaction to yours?' Might as well be blunt.

'I guess. It was easy to say yes because, like you, I believed I wouldn't be needed.' He locked his eyes on hers. 'I'm just being honest.'

Karina shook her head at him. 'You're a great uncle, even agreeing to look out for Mickey. I know James was thrilled. He knew you wouldn't say yes for the hell of it, that you'd have thought it through.'

'It's uncanny that they organised the guardianship only a few months before the accident.' Sadness leaked out of those eyes still focused on her.

'I understand a lot of parents do it these days.' Sadness gripped her as well. 'But you're right—the timing was impeccable.'

'Sounds like my brother. He never left anything to chance.'

At last he looked away, to stare at the wall again. He'd gone from a nightmare to talking about this. *Not good.* Time for her to lighten the mood or neither of them would get any sleep tonight.

'So, tomorrow you're going to gym practice, where the mums will love you.' Maybe she should tag along after all. Huh? Was she feeling a twinge of envy over other women enjoying Logan's company?

'Why?' He looked puzzled.

Didn't he get how good-looking he was? 'A new

man in town never goes amiss.' She dropped her feet to the floor. 'Time I hit the sack.'

Logan's eyes widened, but thankfully he remained quiet.

Shoving herself upright, she headed for the door and solitude. She needed to think about Logan and this funny hitch in her breathing whenever she looked at him.

She didn't want another man in her life. Ian had soured her for that, with his infidelity and his other family on the side; a family he'd seemed more tied to than her. She did owe him in a way, because he'd woken her up to herself and made her see how compliant she was to his demands, which in turn had made it easy for him to control her so thoroughly. Just like her dad had done all her life.

She'd become aware of what she wanted out of her life which was not a grand lifestyle, nor a career-driven one. She'd realised she wanted to earn her own way, make her own decisions whether they be about what to have for dinner or where to live. And here she was. Happy and being strong.

'Goodnight,' she called over her shoulder, and refused to acknowledge the fact that Logan was

watching her as she fled the room. Refused to
admit to that glimmer of heat that had lit up his
eyes when she'd mentioned going to bed.

Neither of them needed to get close to the other.
He obviously had more than enough problems of
his own without adding her to the mix.

Knock, knock. 'Karina? Wake up.'

Karina dragged her eyes open. 'Logan?' *What
now?* Had he had another nightmare? The bedside clock showed five-oh-five.

'Can I come in?'

Her door was already opening.

'Of course.'

Her thick brushed cotton pyjamas gave her all
the decency she could wish for, and would definitely smother any residual heat he might have felt
a few hours ago when she'd left him in the lounge.

She found her bedside light, flicked the switch,
blinked in the sudden yellow glare. 'What's the
problem?'

'We've got a patient waiting in the kitchen.
Steve Garrett.'

'Steve? What's he gone and done this time?'

Logan handed her the robe from the end of her

bed. 'Slipped on ice outside the fish factory and twisted his ankle. He was heading home after the night shift.'

'Ice?' Rain yesterday…frost today. 'At least we'll have a fine day.'

'He seems to be a bit of a toughie. Doesn't want to go to hospital for an X-ray.'

'That's Steve. Hates a fuss. He'll be wanting to get strapped up so as he can go home and get some sleep before he takes over looking after the kids while Faye goes to work.'

Shoving her freezing feet into her slippers she tightened the belt of her robe at her waist, picked up her cell phone and the keys to the surgery and headed for her door, brushing Logan's arm on her way past.

'Welcome to general medicine, Motueka style.'

Logan strode along beside her. 'I was surprised when I opened the door to his knocking.'

'How come you heard him and I didn't?' So much for thinking she was a light sleeper.

'I was still in the lounge.'

So he hadn't gone back to bed. 'Hope you kept the fire going. Eighty-year-old houses lose their heat real fast.'

Shouldn't have said that. He'd file that small piece of info away to bring out when their arguments over selling or not selling stalled.

Steve sat at the dining table, his face screwed in pain as he stared belligerently at his right foot. He looked up the moment they walked into the room. 'Sorry to barge in like this, but you know how it is.'

'Sure do. How are all those kids? Keeping you busy?'

'Running me ragged, more like. Can you strap this foot so's I can work tonight?' He straightened up on the chair, sucked in a sharp breath. 'I'm not feeling so flash.'

'What's not right? Something apart from your ankle?' She pulled out another chair. 'Put your foot on that.'

'My chest hurts when I breathe deep.'

'Tell us more about that tumble you took.' Logan picked up Steve's arm, placed his finger on his wrist and began taking a pulse.

'Not much to tell. One moment I was walking to the car, the next I was flat on my back. My right side's sore. Must've landed that way.'

'You didn't twist sideways? Hit your chest or

shoulder?' Karina asked as Logan continued counting the pulse rate. 'You might've pulled a muscle around your ribs.'

'Could've. I don't know.' Steve held his breath as she began levering his boot off.

'Sorry. This is going to hurt a bit.'

'Just do it.'

Logan stopped counting. 'Pulse is fine. Let me look at your eyes. Pupils all good. Karina, can I get a stethoscope from the surgery? I'd like to be certain that we're only looking at a pulled intercostal muscle.'

'Let's move over there. We're going to need tape to strap this ankle anyway.' Karina crossed to the door that led through to the surgery and tugged the keys from her pocket. 'Leave this open in case Mickey calls out.'

'You really should have an X-ray,' Logan told Steve once they were settled in the nurse's room.

'I walked on it to get here, didn't I?'

'You call that walking? I've seen ducks crossing the road more elegantly than the way you hobbled through here.'

Karina opened the store cupboard to retrieve a roll of elasticised tape.

Logan nodded at Steve. 'I'm not going to ask how you got to the house. It's best I don't know that you drove that vehicle I heard pulling up at the gate minutes before you banged the front door down. But I'm thinking you're right—a broken bone would be giving you far more grief.'

Karina began winding the tape around Steve's swollen ankle and foot. 'If you change your mind, give the surgery a call and David will organise an X-ray in Nelson.'

'Pull your jersey and your shirt up,' Logan instructed when he'd found the stethoscope. He listened to Steve's heart, then gently felt his ribs and sternum. He was thorough and careful. 'Does it hurt when I touch here? Or here?'

Steve shook his head. 'No. Only when I breathe deep, so I'll give up breathing for a bit.'

'Good idea. Do you want some painkillers to see you through the day?' Logan put the stethoscope down on the desk.

'No, I'll be right, thanks, Doc.'

A small smile lifted the corners of Logan's mouth. 'You do realise that the treatment for a sprained ankle is to keep it raised for at least a couple of days?'

'Yeah, sure. No problem.'

Karina chuckled. 'Which means you'll carry on as usual.'

'You honestly think my kids are going to let me lounge around all day?' Steve shook his head at them. 'You have no idea. They'll be running wild within minutes if they know I can't catch them.'

Karina shivered in the doorway as she watched Logan walk down the drive with Steve, ready to grab him if he slipped again. Not that Logan would necessarily stay upright himself if that happened. Jack Frost had been heavy-handed this morning, leaving a thick layer of glistening ice. Mickey would have a blast later, jumping on all those puddles in the lawn to smash the ice layer on top.

Walking back to the kitchen, she looked down at herself and smiled. With her pyjamas and slippers she definitely didn't look elegant—something she'd used to be known for. Funny how in Auckland she'd never even owned a pair of pyjamas, preferring instead lacy negligees, and yet here she didn't care a scrap for anything that wasn't warm and practical for getting up to Mickey.

It went to show how removed from life as she'd

known it she'd become. Had she spent too long here, hiding away, not being forced to partake in that relentless round of socialising her family was famous for? Who cared? She was very happy with her lot.

She certainly didn't miss having to have her make-up on, her hair styled, and being dressed immaculately before Ian got up.

She heard the front door close. Logan had returned. She'd liked watching him in doctor mode: so gentle and careful, yet thorough. He could no more help himself when it came to looking out for someone than she could stop worrying about where to find those thousands of dollars she needed.

What had gone wrong to cause his nightmares? Because she knew as sure as she knew that Mickey was four that he'd had others. While he'd been distressed when she'd woken him, he hadn't been shocked. Once he'd come out of it he'd known what to do to get back to reality quickly.

If only there was a way she could help... But even if there was, Logan wouldn't let her near. He stood tall and proud, and just acknowledging that she'd witnessed him in that distressed state must be annoying the hell out of him.

Logan shook his head. Motueka wasn't the sleepy hollow he'd expected. He still couldn't get his head around Steve just knocking on the door, though it made sense in a roundabout way, with the only alternative being a long drive to the Nelson Emergency Department.

Steve had told him Karina had delivered their last baby after his wife's waters had broken while they were at the park. Karina had been there. The baby had been in a hurry and she'd stepped up.

'She's one in a million, Doc. Don't you go messing with her or talking her into leaving.'

He'd told Steve, 'I'm not taking Karina anywhere.'

Karina would never consider leaving Motueka. She didn't even want to shift to another house, warmer and easier to look after. In her mind Mickey belonged here.

What was it like, knowing where you'd be in twelve months' time? In twenty-four? What was it like waking up in the same house, with the same person, day in, day out, month after month? To feel safe all the time? He guessed he'd never know. Not while there were so many people who needed him back in Africa.

In the kitchen, Karina had switched the kettle on. 'Tea and toast, I reckon. It's not worth going back to bed now. Mr Grumpy will be over soon.'

A wave of guilt rolled through Logan. He'd been one reason she'd lost sleep. A motel for the rest of his stay would be best, but he couldn't find any enthusiasm for the idea.

'It's barely gone six. What's Jonty doing out and about at this hour?'

'He used to be an apple orchardist, and they're always up before the sparrows, especially in spraying season, when they need to be ahead of the wind. Old habits haven't gone away just because he's now living in town.'

She tugged the fridge open, peered inside.

'I guess…'

He still woke before four every morning himself, as he had in Africa. Back in New Zealand, in the deep of winter, he still couldn't get past that hour. If he went to sleep at all. Knowing no one would attack him in the middle of the night didn't mean he sometimes didn't lie awake, waiting for it to happen.

'I know it's early, but do you feel like poached eggs on toast? I've got the munchies.' Karina raised an eyebrow in his direction.

'I'm starving.'

Another habit he hadn't ditched: eating whenever he could because he didn't know when his next meal might turn up. The shrink he'd seen a few times after being released had told him that would eventually change back to normal, once his brain accepted that all the food he could possibly need was available any time he wanted it.

'Where do you put it all?' Karina asked, her eyes skating across his body.

Of course she'd seen him half naked and knew how thin he was under the loose sweatshirt.

He forced a grin. 'I got lucky when metabolisms were being handed out. Mine's fast and furious.'

'Sure.'

So she didn't believe him? *Sorry, that's the best you're going to get, lady.* But he'd give her a half-truth. 'Working in some of the places I do, you soon learn to grab whatever's on offer because there can be many hours between meals if it's chaotic—which it usually is.'

'Why Africa?' She collected eggs and bread, got out a pan and filled it with hot water and added a splash of vinegar. 'It's a long way from home.'

'I went to England first.' *Why had he said that?* 'My mum's English.' *Motor-mouth. Stop.* She'd met Mum, so would know that. 'I have a British passport and I decided to do some post-grad work in London.' *Oh, hell.*

'I didn't know that.'

Why would she? 'Don't tell me you and James never had any heart-to-hearts about his wayward brother?'

Her cheeks reddened, making her prettier than ever. 'He talked about you sometimes; usually after too many whiskies.'

'Ouch.' Logan sucked in air through gritted teeth.

Karina laid a hand on his shoulder. 'Don't take that as a poke for not being around. James knew you were doing what you loved.'

She looked so earnest, so concerned for him. Not to mention downright cute, all wrapped up in her thick robe and with those fluffy slippers that looked like stuffed possums on her feet. He felt his body tilting towards her, as if he were being drawn into a vortex. A vortex he had no idea how he'd get out of if he fell over the edge.

He pulled back a step. Then another. And soon there was enough distance between them for him to stop being so distracted.

She'd turned away to drop bread in the toaster. He watched her hungrily. Every movement, every breath. She was beautiful. Not so much in the traditional physical sense of the word, but in her heart. In the way she helped others, always giving, sharing, trying to allay anxieties. She'd smoothed away his guilt over James, for now at least. She was very dangerous to his equilibrium.

Another step back. 'Thank you for telling me that.'

'How many eggs?'

'Two.' He opened a cupboard and found the biggest array of tea he'd ever seen. 'Which flavour do you want?'

'Plain old gumboot variety, first thing.'

Her lips lifted into a soft smile. And turned his stomach into a riot. *Get over yourself. The woman only smiled, like she does with everyone.*

'Gumboot tea.' He dredged up a chuckle. 'My grandma used to call it that.'

'So did mine. She made pots of tea so stewed you could stand a spoon in it.' She shuddered.

'What time does Mickey get up?'

'After seven. Fingers crossed.'

'It's all go from then on?'

'He's got more energy than I know what to do with. Thank goodness.'

'You worry about his health?'

He placed two mugs at the breakfast bar and went to the drawer to get the cutlery out. Why wouldn't she worry? She'd recently lost her best friend. She understood the precariousness of life. Was that the real reason why she didn't want to move? Had she hidden herself away here?

'Too much, probably. Down syndrome brings its own set of problems.' She winced. 'He's been lucky so far. I'm probably looking for trouble we don't need.'

Seemed that was second nature to her. 'I know he had to have heart surgery for Persistent Ductus Arteriosus soon after he was born. While James sat at Mickey's bedside he often emailed me about his terror that his boy wouldn't survive the aftereffects of the operation.' He'd felt close to James then, wishing he could help in some way.

'Poor little mite. It must've been hideous. Thankfully there've been no lasting problems.'

'You could consider he's had his share of complications pertinent to the condition and now he's got a straight run ahead of him?'

Karina's eyes met his. 'You reckon? Not very medically technical, that approach.'

'No, and nor is worrying about what he *might* get.'

She smiled. 'Thank you. Glad to have you on my side. Now, enjoy your breakfast.'

'Kar—ina.' An ear-shattering yell came from down the hall. 'I'm up!'

Her eye roll was over-the-top and funny.

'So much for seven o'clock.' She pushed her breakfast aside and stood.

Logan leapt up and pressed a hand on her shoulder, pushed downwards until she sat. 'Let me get him. You eat your eggs.'

The surprise on her face was worth the million questions rolling through his tired brain about what to do with Mickey.

'Just give me a few pointers. Do I get him

dressed for the day or are dressing gown and slippers all right for now?'

She shook her head as she smiled. 'Mickey will let you know.'

CHAPTER FIVE

ON HER WAY back to work after lunch two days later, Karina diverted to the driveway to take a nosy at the hole Logan had managed to make many times bigger than the mere nuisance it had previously been.

'What was wrong with filling it with some of that gravel piled out the back?'

'Don't interfere with a man's work,' Jonty growled as he struggled to shovel dirt into a barrow.

Logan stopped digging and wiped the back of his hand over his damp forehead. Why did he do that? It was diverting; it drew her gaze to his mud-smeared face. He looked exhausted and had done since first thing that morning, when she'd found him in the kitchen making porridge.

'Something I remember from childhood. Gran's oats covered in brown sugar and cream.'

When he'd smacked his lips she'd wanted to

laugh, but the breath had hitched in her throat as his tongue had slid across his bottom lip. She'd had to turn away and look for the bread to make Mickey's toast, otherwise she'd have reached across and traced the outline of his mouth. That would have been just great for ongoing relations.

As far as she knew he hadn't had a nightmare last night. But judging by the shadows under his eyes he must have sat up all night trying to hold them in abeyance. He couldn't keep doing that. She'd explain later that it was okay if he woke her. Not that he'd like that one little bit.

Logan caught her attention. 'There's a drainage problem that's caused seepage. That in turn has undermined the driveway. We're fixing it properly to prevent it happening again.'

What was wrong with it just being a hole that filled with water every time it rained?

'It's grown a bit bigger every time we've had heavy rain, but it's not like it's a huge problem.' *Yet.*

'Relax, Karina. Jonty and I'll get it sorted. It's not going to cost you a thing.'

So he knew where her real concern lay. Of course he did. Hadn't her visit to the bank been the subject of their very first conversation? 'Thanks.' *I think.*

Then Jonty got in on the act. 'When are you taking your car in for those tyres?'

Damn him for asking in front of Logan. Keep this up and Logan would be thinking she was too incompetent to be raising his nephew. If he didn't already.

'I'll get around to it over the next few days. No hurry.'

Except she needed to get the groceries in, and there was a trailer-load of firewood to be collected from Becca's brother's place.

Logan folded his hands across the end of the shovel handle and dropped his chin on top. 'You shouldn't leave your car unroadworthy. What if something happens to Mickey? What if it's raining when you take him to gym practice?'

'Haven't you got a vehicle somewhere we could use? Don't tell me you came over by bus?'

'Yes, I have a rental four-wheel drive. It's parked outside the gate.'

She'd seen the vehicle by the kerbside for a few days but hadn't thought anything of it. 'Good. Have I got some chores for *you*!'

I'll ignore that smile that's got my knickers in a twist. What was it about this man that had her hormones sitting up and taking notice when she definitely didn't want to be interested? Who was in charge of her body's reactions anyway? Logan or her?

He shrugged and banged the shovel into the hole. 'Sure. Any time.'

Nothing wrong with his hormones, then.

Jonty had been standing there listening to this conversation, his eyes flicking between her and Logan, a hint of mischief in his gaze. As he opened his mouth, Karina wanted to put her hand across it to stop whatever he was about to say. But he surprised her into silence.

'Get your car along to the tyre shop on Greenwood Street tomorrow and my nephew will change the tyres.'

'I'll arrange a time later. Thanks, Jonty.' *After pay day next week.*

Jonty was pulling his cell out of his pocket and punching some numbers. 'Tomorrow,' he growled at her. 'Kevin—Karina's car needs some tyres for her warrant. Do it tomorrow, will you? Yep. I'll tell her. Put it on my account.' Snap. The phone was off. 'He'll pick it up before he opens at eight.'

'Jonty, you can't go paying for my tyres.' How embarrassing. Her eyes shifted sideways, locked with Logan's steady grey gaze. There was no condemnation there, only understanding.

Jonty growled. 'I'll pay for whatever I like. Before eight o'clock. Don't forget.'

'I won't.' She reached over and wrapped her arms around the generous old man. 'Thank you so much.'

Jonty pulled out of her hug. 'Don't get all silly, girl. It's only so as you can get supplies in for our dinners.'

She laughed. 'Then I'll make your favourite pudding for tomorrow night.'

Logan paused with a shovelful of mud and stones. 'Can I ask what that might be?'

'Apple and raspberry pie with lashings of ice cream.' She'd picked and frozen raspberries from the garden during summer, so that there would be a steady stream of pies over winter.

Logan winked at her. 'Vanilla ice cream?'

'If you're lucky,' she said. 'I'd better get to work before they send out a search party. Jonty?' She tapped her friend's shoulder. 'I really do appreciate what you're doing for me.'

'Get to work, girl, and stop your blathering.'

Jonty and Logan were laughing together as she crossed the lawn. Now that he'd retired Jonty must miss male companionship after years of employing many local men.

Mickey seemed to have hit on the male bonding thing too. It had been almost impossible to drag him away from the men and inside for lunch. And when it had come time to go to kindergarten he'd refused, thrown a rare tantrum. That had startled Karina into giving in far too easily. She was torn between being consistent in her parenting and letting him spend time with Uncle Logan. Tomorrow she'd get him back on track.

Karina sighed away a sense of being on the outside of things. The guys were happy doing man stuff. Nothing to get her knickers in a knot about.

Walking into the clinic, Karina made for the nurses' room, only to pause at the door of David's consulting room. 'Hi. Are you all right?'

David was behind his desk, leaning with his forehead in his hands. The face he turned towards her was green. 'Not really.'

Crossing to him, she was startled to see his rubbish bin placed strategically at his feet. 'Want to throw up, do you?'

'Yep.'

'What else? A fever? Stomach cramps?' Her hand touched his forehead. 'You've got a temperature.'

'My kids came home from school the day before yesterday with the *D*s and *V*s. Guess they've passed it on.' He groaned and held his breath. Then said, 'It was so sudden. I was fine before lunch.'

'What did you have for lunch?'

'Pumpkin soup and toast.' He shook his head carefully. 'Not the culprit.'

'Guess not. You'd better go home and get into bed. If you stay here you'll pass it on to patients and staff.'

What about the patients he'd seen earlier? Had they already caught the bug?

'The waiting room's full.' David groaned again.

'I'll ask Logan to fill in for you. After I've phoned your wife to come get you.'

'She can't leave the kids home alone.' He

reached for the bin and Karina stepped back as
he heaved.

'Then I'll take you. Just stay in here until I get
back.' She placed a box of antiseptic-infused tis-
sues on the desk at his elbow. 'I'll be as quick as
I can.'

Back outside, she called, 'Logan, we've got a
problem. David's been taken ill and the patients
are backing up already. Can you help out?'

He was a partner in the clinic, after all.

'Sure. Sorry, Jonty, we'll have to leave this for
now.' Already Logan had placed the shovel on
top of the wheelbarrow and was striding towards
the house. 'Karina, tell David I'll be there in ten
minutes. I need to clean up and change into something a little more presentable.'

'Mickey, you're going to have to go to kindy
now. Uncle Logan's going to work.'

'No!' Mickey screamed, and ran to hide in the
garden shed.

'What's that about?' Karina stared after him.

Logan shrugged. 'I'd say he's happier playing
at home, that's all.'

Jonty headed for the shed. 'I'll sort him. You
get him some clean clothes.'

Karina followed Logan to the back door. 'Can I use the four-wheel drive to take David home?'

'Keys are on my bed.' He sat on the top step at the back door to tug off the now filthy work boots that had used to belong to James. 'What's David's problem?' he asked as she stepped past him.

'Probably a twenty-four-hour tummy bug. He says his children came home with it two days ago. I did hear about something doing the rounds yesterday, but this is the first I've seen of it. I hope Mickey hasn't caught it from one of his play-mates.'

'Nothing wrong with his energy levels all morning.' Logan stood up and went inside in his damp socks, leaving wet footprints on the clean vinyl of the laundry floor and all the way through the kitchen.

Karina pulled a face at his back. She'd washed the floors only that morning, before going to work, and now there was a trail of size-twelve outlines cutting across the middle of them. She guessed that was what having a man living in the house meant.

Mickey fought her as she removed his soiled

clothing and pulled on a new set. 'Why can't I
stay with Mr Grumpy?'

'Because I said so.' *Huh?* She glanced over her
shoulder, looking for her mother, who'd used that
exact expression and tone to her so often as she
was growing up.

Wherever the words came from, they worked.
Mickey quietened down and helped pull his sweatshirt on. When his head popped through the top
she grabbed him into a hug, placed a hand on his
forehead to check his temperature and gave him
a kiss.

'That's my boy.'

When Karina returned to the medical centre
after dropping David and Mickey at their desti-
nations, she found everyone quietly waiting for
their turn with Logan. According to Leeann, the
receptionist, he'd explained the situation to them
and was now busy familiarising himself with the
computer system in the consulting room.

Leeann had made tea and coffee for those patients who wanted it. 'Keeping them happy!' She
grinned at Karina.

'Go, you.'

She found Logan in David's room.

'Anything you need a hand with?' she asked.

'I can't find the lab forms.' His brow was furrowed, making him look studious. He'd scrubbed up darned well, looking very debonair in a crisp white shirt.

Leaning over his shoulder, she showed him which file he needed and watched until he opened it. His hair, hanging over his collar, was damp from his hurried shower. He smelled of soap. How she managed not to run her hand over his head she'd never know. Stepping back quickly, she drew oxygen into her lungs and tried to act as if she felt light-headed every day.

'Karina? You're not feeling ill, too?'

The concern in his tone would have been warming if it hadn't embarrassed her because of what she was thinking.

'I'm fine.' When he narrowed his eyes she sped to the door and escape. 'Call me if you need anything.'

She'd be hiding in her room, folding towels and ordering swabs, hoping Logan didn't twig to her completely unprofessional behaviour.

To be reacting to a man at all was unusual for her. To be doing so at work, when he'd stepped in for her colleague, was wrong. Her phone rang, thankfully diverting her from all thoughts of Logan and on to laboratory results.

The problem with that was hearing that young Sarah Griggs's haemoglobin was far too low, and the blood film suggested severe iron deficiency. Now Karina had to discuss this with Logan in between John Gainsborough getting a repeat prescription for statins and Colleen Murphy limping badly from a pulled muscle at the back of her knee after a rough netball game.

'The lab's running tests on Sarah's blood for iron levels and will send them through the moment they're ready,' she told him.

'With a haemoglobin of seventy she needs a blood transfusion, not to mention finding the cause of her anaemia.' Logan brought up Sarah's file on the screen. 'She doesn't appear to have any previous history of iron deficiency. I wonder what her diet's like? She seems too young for a bleeding ulcer, but it's not impossible.'

He ran through the options and asked a couple of questions about whom to contact at the hospital for follow-up tests.

After showing him the contacts list, Karina

said, 'I'll tell your next patient there'll be another delay.'

Logan had to phone Sarah's mother pronto.

The afternoon progressed with everyone feeling they were continuously taking two steps forward and one back. By the time Logan saw his last patient out, Karina knew he was shattered. Those shadows under his eyes were now big black patches, while the lines defining the corners of his mouth appeared deeper. Her heart squeezed. Lack of sleep was catching up with him.

Quietly she said, 'Time to lock up and go see Mickey. He'll be beside himself with wanting to be with us.'

Jonty had collected him from kindy and was staying with him.

Logan's dark, thick eyebrows rose as if she'd made a blunder, but all he said was, 'I'm surprised he hasn't been banging the door down to get in here to find his Karina.'

'And his Uncle Logan.'

'He hasn't called me that yet. I doubt he understands the concept of what an uncle is.'

Karina nudged him towards the door. 'Let's get out of here before the phone rings again.'

It had been quiet for at least five minutes. Unbelievable.

Punching in the security code, she told him, 'Mickey knows more than you realise. James spent a lot of time explaining where you fitted into his family.'

'Of course he did. What was I thinking?'

He tried to stifle a yawn, but in the light flooding the yard from the high-intensity security lights Karina saw the telltale strain of his mouth and jaw.

She slipped her arm through his and headed for the back door. 'Roast chicken for dinner. Hope you like it?'

'Sounds delicious. I haven't had a roast for years.' He pressed her arm against his side. 'Why are we out here when you've got an internal door between the surgery and the private part of the house?'

'The insurance company demands that door stays locked. Anyway, I prefer keeping both domains separate. Home and work.'

'Fair enough.' He opened the back door and

stepped back as Mickey rushed past him and leapt at her.

'Kar—ina, where've you been? I don't like kindy any more.'

Whoomph. Karina gasped and staggered backwards as a tornado of arms and legs wrapped around her. 'Sweetheart—steady.'

What was this about kindy? Usually he couldn't wait to get there.

'Careful, my boy.' Logan's hand spread across her back, pressing forward to keep her upright. 'You've got to be gentle with ladies.'

'He does?' She blinked up at the man and leaned harder against his warm hand.

He instantly dropped his arm and muttered, 'Basic training in the male-female relationship. Always look out for the lady.'

Thankfully Mickey squirmed to get down just then, distracting her so that she didn't have to think of a reply—if one was needed.

'Logan, can we dig some more on the drive?'

'It's *Uncle* Logan, Mickey. And no, it's too dark and cold to be outside. We'll get back to the job at the weekend.'

'I want to do it now.'

'No, Mickey, we can't.'

'Why not?'

'Because it's late and I'm tired.' Logan's jaw was tense.

Mickey stared at him. 'You have to go to bed.' Then he wandered away to watch TV.

Karina headed for the kitchen, tossing over her shoulder at Logan, 'Go easy on him. He's still trying to get his head around the concept that Mummy and Daddy aren't here to play with him.'

He followed her. 'I'm a doctor, and I understand totally what's happened to them, and I still can't get my head around it. James was thirty-seven, with a son to live for. I'm two years younger and running solo. Life's very unfair.'

'It's incomprehensible.' Without thinking she placed her hand on his forearm, her fingers pressing into his jersey-clad muscles. 'That's how it is at times.'

Logan leaned back to peer down at her. 'You haven't had an easy time of things, have you? In your own life, I mean?'

She couldn't answer around the tears suddenly blocking her throat so she backed away, opened the oven to check on the chicken and the vegetables. Everything was browning perfectly and the succulent smell of roast meat filled the air. Thank goodness for oven timers.

Above her head, Logan murmured, 'I'll set the table.'

'Don't forget Jonty,' she managed.

He was in the lounge, watching the news and keeping an eye on the fire.

'Karina?' Logan hadn't moved away. 'I'm sorry if I've inadvertently upset you.'

Closing the oven door, she headed for the freezer to get a packet of peas. 'No problem.'

Where had those tears come from? It had been a long while since she'd shed tears for her broken marriage. Coming home after a hectic day at work, with Logan beside her, Mickey eager to see her; all had conspired to give her a sense of longing so deep it frightened her. Longing for what she'd once thought she'd have with Ian. Longing to love someone, to be loved in return. A deep yearning for a baby. A family of her own. Which was plain stupid. She had a child—a boy who needed her so much it hurt at times. Mickey was her family.

'It's me who should be apologising. I don't

know where that sadness came from.' *Liar*. She did know; but not why now, here, with Logan. She felt lost. She hadn't done lost for a long time.

Catching her elbow, Logan turned her to face him. 'Don't ever apologise for your emotions. Especially not to me. You are entitled to cry, to feel sad, angry, or whatever grips you at that moment. You don't always have to laugh and smile.'

His rare soft smile said he totally understood. 'Thank you.'

She had to push him away right now, this instant, because with every minute he was moving closer and closer to overtaking her heart.

She straightened her back and stomped to the pot drawer. 'That roast's calling.'

'My stomach just sat up in anticipation,' Logan said on his way past to the laundry with a dirty tea towel. Then he was back, asking, 'How long's the roof been leaking in that room?'

The stains on the ceiling were in varying shades of murky brown from the many times rain had come through. 'Since before I moved in.'

'I'll put that on the list of jobs to do.' He headed to the dining room.

Forget feeling lost—try angry.

'Put it on the list?' She snapped her fingers. 'Just like that. Get the job done; tick it off the blasted list. Call the real estate agent, find a buyer, kick Mickey out of his home. Oh, no, you don't, Logan Pascale. No, you damn well don't.'

'Smells delicious.' Logan placed tablemats on the table, found cutlery and set out four glasses. He was beyond tired and knew if he didn't get some sleep tonight he'd be a basket case tomorrow.

There was no response. Karina seemed too busy stirring the gravy and holding a conversation with herself. What had got her all antsy now?

'Kar—ina. I want a hug,' Mickey demanded. 'I've been good.'

She spun around and her face lit up, banishing the unexpected anger blinking out of those big brown eyes. 'Come here.' Her lips softened into a smile as she hauled Mickey up into her arms.

Logan ached to wrap his arms around them both and hold them close. To protect them. Instead he stepped around them and headed for the room that was temporarily his bedroom to dump his wallet and phone. Their voices and laughter followed him down the hall.

Karina. He'd seen her pain in her tight body, heard it in her tear-filled voice, known it in the desolation echoing through her words. A broken marriage and the loss of Maria would have taken a toll. Throw in the added responsibility for a young boy who wasn't hers and no wonder she had her moments of feeling down. She came across as strong, but occasionally he glimpsed turmoil in her gaze. Was he adding to that by being here? By wanting to improve her situation in his own way?

Logan's hands curled into fists. He cursed the militants who'd kept him from returning in time for the joint funeral. He could have helped Karina—stood by her as she hurt.

He felt sweat beading his brow as once again he ran through the day he'd been kidnapped, searching for anything he could have done so that he might have made it back to New Zealand in time. Again there was no lightbulb moment to show how he could have done anything differently. Face it: with an Uzi jabbed into his back there really hadn't been any other way of reacting except to move in whatever direction he was ordered.

Which only made him more incapable than he'd believed he was. Unable to save himself or either of his colleagues who had also been dragged away to be dumped in huts in the most hostile place he'd ever had the misfortune to be.

'Uncle Logan, here's my storybook.'

Logan blinked, shook his head to block those hideous memories from becoming a full-blown storm in his brain, and dropped to his haunches to eyeball Mickey. 'What did you call me?'

'Uncle Logan. That's who you are.' The boy nodded seriously. 'My daddy's brother.'

'Yes, Mickey, I'm your uncle. How cool's that?' He held his hand up to high-five him. Mickey slapped him in return and warmth stole into Logan's heart for this tough little guy. 'It's cool being uncle and nephew.'

'Do it again.'

'What are we agreeing on this time?'

Mickey's small hand barely covered his palm. 'Everything.'

'I see there's some serious male bonding going on here.' Karina stood in the doorway. 'I hate to break up the fun, but Mickey, you need to wash your hands for dinner.'

'Come on, Uncle Logan. Wash your hands or Karina won't let you eat.'

'Does he get the bossy thing from you, by any chance?' Logan asked as he stood up.

She gave a wary smile. 'Of course.'

'Actually, I think he's got James's genes there.' He casually dropped an arm over her shoulders, half expecting her to pull away.

Which she did. Tugging free to move into the hallway, her face tightening.

'Karina? What's wrong?'

She was definitely going a bit remote on him.

'Not a thing. Truly,' she added when he locked eyes with her. 'I'm wondering how David's getting on and if he'll be at work tomorrow.'

He knew that was quick improvising, but if she wanted the subject changed he'd play the game. 'Why not leave him be? I'll cover for him until he's back on his feet.'

'You realise he'll be getting his hopes up that you might decide to stay on and take his place permanently?'

'When you tell David I'll cover for him again, you can throw in a bit about me heading back to my other job as soon as I'm fit enough.'

Damn, damn, damn. His mouth had got away on him.

'You're not fit?'

Of course she'd instantly pick up on his blunder. '"Worn out" is the non-technical term.'

Would he get away with that?

Her eyes filled with disappointment. 'Sure...' She shrugged. 'I guess it must be exhausting, working in extreme heat and without the usual backup that modern hospitals provide.'

He saw behind her attempt to get him to speak about his life in Africa. She wanted to know why he was unfit, why he had nightmares, why he wasn't rushing back to his job for the next few weeks.

'At least I get down time. Unlike you. You go from one job to the next, never taking time out for yourself.'

'Mickey isn't a job,' she snapped, the disappointment shadowing her eyes quickly replaced with annoyance. 'I'm a normal person, going to work at the medical centre and coming home to look after my boy and do the usual household chores.'

'You've made a haven here, but how long do you think you can go on living like this? Pretending it's normal? Because it's not, whichever way you look at it. You've had someone else's child thrust on you. You've got a medical surgery to keep running and you're not a doctor. And we won't even mention this house.'

Triple damn again. Talk about motor-mouth. Exhaustion did that to him time and again.

Karina snapped, 'You're a fine one to talk. Why do you spend your life in the remotest of locations? Out of touch with your family?'

She leaned back against the wall and folded her arms, pushing those tantalising breasts up and out. Breasts that were rising and falling rapidly as her breathing tempo ramped up. Breasts that pushed at the front of her white blouse and drew his gaze, making him temporarily forget what they were arguing about.

Her foot tapped the carpet. Logan shivered. For a guy who preferred his own company and didn't do heart-to-heart conversations, this strange sense of loss just because Karina had gone quiet on him as she waited for an explanation he couldn't give came out of left field.

She could have rubbed his nose in the fact that half the responsibilities around here were actually his. But she hadn't.

Lifting his eyes, he met her steady gaze. 'I left

New Zealand because I didn't feel connected to anything or anyone.'

No, that wasn't one hundred per cent correct, and somehow he knew Karina would see through any attempts to gloss over things in his usual careless way. Unbelievable, but he found he didn't want to lose credibility with her.

'My family were all busy doing their own thing. I decided to go to London for post-grad work. That's where I heard about the African Health Organisation and immediately applied to work for them. Something clicked. I wanted to help people who were desperate. I've never gone without life's basics, and a part of me has always been about making sure others have the same advantages.'

Her stance softened a fraction. Those arms dropped to her sides and she straightened up again. 'You didn't think you'd be able to help people in your own country?'

'Of course I did. But on the African continent illness and need is on such a huge scale. There's no welfare system for the poor and desperate.'

He pushed away from the bench he'd been leaning against.

'Shouldn't we be feeding Mickey and Jonty?'

'As opposed to telling each other a little about ourselves? Yes, you're probably right. But, Logan, I think you're wrong. There are many people in this country who could do with your skills.'

Logan didn't want to argue with her. 'I'll tell the others dinner's ready.'

He needed to get away from her for a moment—to break that thread of contact that had him telling her things he'd never talked about, not even to the shrink.

What was it about Karina that had him prattling on so much? She didn't need to know about his current situation. Nightmares excepted. She had enough of her own hassles to deal with.

Remember that next time your tongue starts getting away on you, Logan. Forget that at your peril.

Telling Karina the nitty-gritty of his life was allowing her too close—something neither of them needed.

So when he returned to the dining table with Mickey in hand he said something that would keep her at a distance. 'Have you ever thought about where you might like to live if this place sells?'

'Not once.'

'I hear there are some new subdivisions going on, with big homes being planned.'

'I've got a big home.'

Ice would have been warmer.

Logan deliberately dug a bigger hole. 'A sprawling, ramshackle building that needs painting, insulating and refurbishing?'

'Mickey, don't put your knife in your mouth.' Karina watched the boy with an eagle eye, and totally ignored Logan.

Jonty concentrated entirely on eating, shovelling his food in as though he didn't know when he'd next eat.

Logan forked up a mouthful of chicken and mushroom and chewed thoughtfully. The problem with getting what he wanted was that it wouldn't necessarily make him any happier. Less so in this instance. He had pushed Karina away, but now he desperately wanted her back on side, laughing with him, not looking at him as if he intended stealing the roof from over the head of the person she loved.

His belly soured. He knew with absolute certainty that he'd hurt Karina if he carried on with his plan before coming up with a better idea for her future—one that suited her. Even he finally understood that she meant it when she said she wasn't leaving easily.

He had some serious thinking to do.

After dinner.

As a yawn opened his mouth he grimaced. Make that after a good night's sleep.

At least with this level of tiredness he should manage to sleep right through and not have a nightmare.

But then Jonty joined in, first banging his knife and fork down on his now empty plate, then asking, 'What are you up to, Pascale? Selling? Over my dead body, lad.'

Logan swallowed his mouthful. The day just kept on getting better and better.

CHAPTER SIX

'GET AWAY FROM ME,' Logan snarled.

The gun barrel was whipped across his back. Shafts of pain zapped through his body. No one believed in moderation around here. The only language these men used was violence.

'I need the toilet. Get it? Moron…' Logan muttered under his breath.

A large man shoved at his shoulder hard, so he stumbled against a tree. Pain grabbed his calf muscle, where a wound from a machete festered.

'Don't touch me!' Logan spat at his assailant.

A hand gripped his forearm, shook him. 'Logan.'

'Ah! You've finally learned my name. Leave me alone.'

'Logan.'

That pesky voice persisted.

'Logan, wake up. You're having a nightmare.'

What else could being used as a punch bag by these thugs be?

'It's me, Karina. You're safe. You're at James's house. Wake up.'

The shaking at his forearm grew stronger, more insistent. He opened his eyes barely enough to see what was going on. Karina? A nightmare?

Reality slammed in. Another nightmare.

Slowly, slowly, the evil in his skull faded and he felt safe enough to open his eyes fully. Karina sat on a low stool beside his bed, her hand still holding his arm. Her lovely face oozed concern. In the half-light from the hall she appeared smaller, softer, less than the energy-packed woman she really was.

He shoved upwards to sit with his back against the pillow. Sweat rolled between his shoulder blades, poured from his brow into his eyes, the salt stinging.

'I got you up again.'

Her smile was blinding because it was for him. 'No, Mickey did that. He needed to go pee-pee. Too much water before he went to bed.'

'Thanks for waking me.'

He'd deliberately sat up most of the previous night so he'd be so tired tonight he wouldn't have a nightmare. Showed how much he knew.

'Want a hot chocolate?' asked the soft voice that banished the harsher ones in his head.

'Love one.'

'I'll be right back.'

Karina leapt up and headed for the kitchen, taking the warmth with her.

Logan shivered, ran his hands up and down his arms, trying to heat his icy skin. When that didn't work he scooped up his sweatshirt from the floor and pulled it on before finding his jeans. He was done with sleeping.

'Why are you getting up?' Karina asked from the doorway.

He glanced over his shoulder at her. 'I always do when this happens.'

Her eyes were wide as she stared at him. Make that as she stared at his backside, if the direction of her startled gaze was anything to go by. So she'd got an eyeful? Didn't look as if she thought the sight was too bad.

She lifted her head and locked on his eyes. Her cheeks heated up a cute shade of pink. 'Um…that milk will be ready.'

She was gone, her feet slapping the carpet as

she ran down the hall. She'd left the milk heating unwatched? That was unlike Karina.

He followed, stopping when he saw her making her tea, not his chocolate. That sat waiting, ready, on the bench. So she hadn't left the milk where it could boil over.

The tension in his gut began backing off. He'd got under that smooth skin and tipped her world a little bit upside down. Cool. He liked that.

Whoa. No, he didn't. What had happened to staying clear of all involvement? Hadn't he talked himself through this earlier in the day? He could not afford to get close to Karina in any context of the word.

Pulling on an unemotional, uninvolved, just-a-friend kind of face, he picked up the mug of chocolate and watched as she dunked the teabag again and again.

'That's going to taste revolting if you keep mauling that bag.'

Flick. The teabag and the teaspoon landed in the sink. 'You should go back to bed with your drink. It might relax you enough to fall asleep.'

Exactly. He wasn't ready for another round with the guerrillas. 'Think I'll sit by the fire for a bit.'

Nodding, as if she'd expected him to say that, Karina headed for the big room. 'I'll throw some wood on the fire.'

Following slowly, he sipped his chocolate and watched the sway of her hips under that thick robe. He relaxed some more. She did that to him without even trying.

When she'd finished stoking the fire she turned to him with a smile and he said, 'I like it when you smile.' It warmed him and curled his toes. Not to mention tightened his groin.

The situation just kept getting more complex by the day. So he shouldn't now be running his finger down one of those bewitching pink cheeks.

'I'll make a deal with you. I'll smile more if you do. At least ten times a day.'

Putting his mug aside, he reached to cup her chin, tipped her head back further, all the better to see every expression flitting across her face. 'I don't smile enough?'

'Nope.' She'd stopped smiling. Instead she looked sad. For him?

He bent his head closer to that tantalising mouth, grazed his lips across hers. 'I'll try harder,' he murmured.

Karina whispered something he didn't catch as he touched her mouth with his, pressing harder this time. She obviously hadn't said stop, because right at this moment she was pushing her warm body against his hungry one.

He responded by increasing the pressure of his kiss, and when her mouth opened under his he slipped his tongue inside that sweet cavern and tasted her. When Karina danced her tongue across and around his mouth he lost all sense of everything except this wonderful woman his arms were suddenly wound around. She was exquisite: delicate yet strong, soft yet fiery, sweet yet acid.

A low growl slid across his bottom lip. Karina jerked back, taking that sumptuous mouth with her. Her eyes were filled with some strange emotion he didn't dare put a name to in case it echoed his own need. Her tongue traced her lips where moments ago his mouth had been, as though she was savouring him.

Then she tamped down hard on all his heat and the sensations racing through his body.

'Logan, we can't do this.'

'You're right—we can't.'

But they just had, and he wasn't ready to stop, no matter how sane and sensible that might be.

She continued as though he hadn't spoken. 'It won't solve a thing. Will make everything worse, if anything. We want different outcomes with this house, with Mickey's living arrangements, with my life. We need to keep talking, get to know each other so we understand where we're both coming from and where we're headed.'

She dropped into one of the armchairs.

Damn, she was so right in one way. But he sought oblivion from the nightmares and where better than in Karina's arms? Unfortunately it seemed Karina could haul the brakes on far easier than him.

'I was getting to know you just then.'

He sat opposite her. His mouth still felt the impression of her lips, still tasted her. Still wanted more of her.

Her face hardened. 'Don't be flip.'

'I wasn't. That's how I feel.'

'Tell me about your nightmares.'

Restless, he stood up to move closer to the fire. His skin still held a chill, his feet needed to be moving.

Karina sipped her tea, both hands wrapped around the mug. 'You said something about a gun the other night. Tonight you swore and mentioned going into your hut. You were very angry.'

She'd got that right. Angry and unable to do a damned thing about it. Not during the nightmare, nor when it had been for real. He'd been caught up in something so big it had been terrifying. The vulnerability he'd known had unnerved him. No wonder he got angry. That worried him. Sure, he could get fired up, like anyone, but it was always short-lived. It wasn't this gut-deep, almost out-of-control conflagration that consumed him.

Another sip of tea and she was saying quietly, 'Have you talked to someone about them?'

Them? The nightmares? Or the men who'd done this to him? The shrink had told him only time and talking would help. The horror was locked in his head, sometimes getting as far as his throat, where it blocked off all the words pushing to spew out. Except when he slept. Then he seemed to be able to articulate some of his anger.

'Yes.'

'Did it help?'

'No.'

Yet sitting here with Karina, watching her as she relaxed into her chair, he could feel the red-hot coils in his gut loosening, cooling. She'd done him more good than anyone else had.

The next words he uttered slipped out before he'd finished thinking them. 'You've got the biggest heart I've ever known.'

'That's one way of telling me to mind my own business.' After a long moment she said tiredly, 'I think it's time I tried to get some sleep.'

As in going to bed. Her bed. Alone. Where he couldn't hold her or kiss her. Wise woman.

'Karina?' he called softly as she reached the door. 'I'm not ready to talk. Yet.'

But maybe the day would come when he could—with her.

Karina slid into bed and punched the pillow so it would mould around her neck and keep the cool air out. Closing her eyes, she waited for the sleep she doubted was there for her.

She'd pushed Logan too hard with her questions, as though his kiss had given her the right. Her fingertip outlined her bottom lip. *Why did I stop kissing him?*

Because there was too much between them—too much in his past, too much everything—to be getting so close to each other. Because, for her, a kiss was more than a smacking of lips. Kissing a man meant something. That man had to touch her in some indefinable way—and Logan did exactly that.

Considering her stance on men these days, her reaction didn't fit with her need to be independent. And from the few things he'd let slip she doubted Logan wanted a long-term relationship.

His silences were full of stop signals, and yet she kept finding another question to ask, and another. The guy hurt so badly at times that the pain poured out of him. When he came out of those nightmares his eyes glittered with anger and fear and vulnerability. He'd hate it that she saw the vulnerability. He was a man's man. He took pride in his strength, wouldn't expect to be bested by anyone. Yet she knew someone had got the better of him.

Who? Why? Where? In Africa, obviously, because he'd only been back in New Zealand a week and this wasn't new. He had the jaded appearance

of a man who'd been through these nightmares
many times.

From that blank expression when she'd asked
about them, she wasn't about to find out anything
enlightening any time soon, if at all. Everyone
was entitled to privacy, but her heart ached to be
able to share, to take away some of that pain.

Not going to happen.

And that kiss...? Her lips softened as her forefinger again traced their outline. As far as kisses
went it hadn't been earth-shattering, but it had
been damned close. Logan's mouth on hers had
warmed her right to the tips of her toes and made
her happy. And excited. For someone intent on a
solo life her world had been tipped sideways in a
very disturbing way.

'Kar—ina.'

Mickey.

She sighed as she shoved herself out of bed and
groped around in the dark for her slippers and
dressing gown. Mickey was quite capable of going
to the bathroom on his own. The hall nightlight
kept darkness at bay.

'Coming, sweetheart,' she called quietly.

'I need pee-pee.' Mickey was rubbing his eyes

with his fists and looking absolutely adorable when she flicked his bedside light on.

'You'll have to cut back on drinks before bed-time if you're going to keep waking up like this.'

Once in the bathroom, Mickey was happy for her to go and straighten up the mess that was his bed. A restless sleeper, Mickey always managed to tangle his sheets and duvet, and to lose his pil-low down behind the headboard.

'I'm finished.' Mickey appeared at her side. 'I want a drink of water.'

'Not a good idea. You'll want to go pee-pee again.'

'I'm thirsty.'

'How thirsty?' She felt his brow. No tempera-ture. His face was its usual colour. Had he con-tracted that tummy bug? 'Do you feel all right?'

'Yes, very good. Can I have my water now?'

'Get into bed and I'll get it. A very small glass.'

Along the hall she peeked into the lounge and spied Logan, sprawled out in the armchair, those long legs stretched close to the firebox. A gentle snoring filled the quiet.

'Not returning to your bed again?' she whispered. 'Is this your way of fighting the night-mare's return?'

What would he do if she kissed his cheek or brow, like she did Mickey? She'd never know.

Returning to Mickey's room, she found him sound asleep. Tucking the sheets up over his shoulders, she gazed down at him. He was so cute it broke her heart. So far he hadn't had to deal with any trouble from other kids about his Down syndrome, but the day would come and she wanted him to be strong and happy, so that he could cope with any teasing he might encounter.

Back in bed, she let her worries about finding the money to buy out Logan fill her mind. What with David getting ill and the surgery overly busy, she hadn't got around to phoning any other banks to make appointments with their managers. She'd start first thing in the morning. If that failed she'd have to come up with another solution.

Like what? her brain taunted.

The most obvious answer would be to call her father and tell him she would use some of her trust fund after all. But, despite having a sensible reason to do that, she wouldn't. It would be tantamount to admitting she couldn't manage without her family's wealth. No. She'd find another way.

'Pee-pee, Karina.'

Alarm bells began beeping. Mickey used to have urinary infections regularly, but not lately. Three times in one night was not like him. Did he have an infection? Poor little man didn't deserve one.

It was nearly six and there didn't seem any point trying to snaffle half an hour's shut-eye. In the kitchen she made a cup of tea and sat at the table, opening yesterday's mail. The power bill was higher than usual, but then she did use the clothes dryer during winter. The rates bill was there. Thank goodness for Jonty taking care of her tyres. He'd saved her heaps.

Maybe Mr Bank Manager did have a point. She *wasn't* a good risk for a loan. But she could and would always pay her way, no matter how hard it got. Coming from a background of endless money to spend on absolutely anything that took her fancy, learning to save should have been difficult for her, but it hadn't. In Motueka she didn't need loads of new clothes, didn't go tripping off on exotic holidays. Life had become simple, and she loved it.

Sure, there had been days when it had frustrated her that she couldn't just hop on a plane to somewhere warm, or cool, or whatever her mood wanted at the time. But she'd soon learned she didn't need any of that to make her feel good about herself. Realising that Ian had had too much control over her and she was now free had done that.

But right now she did need money, and she wasn't as free she'd like. She was tied to doing what Logan expected if she didn't find that pot of gold, didn't make him see there were other solutions than the one he was hell-bent on.

'Hey, you're up early.' Logan strolled into the room, looking all mussed up.

'I think Mickey's got a urinary infection. He's been up to the bathroom three times.'

'I'll check him over when he next wakes up. He hasn't got a fever, has he?'

She shook her head. 'Didn't seem to.'

'Has he had an infection before?'

'A while back.'

'Okay.' Logan filled the kettle and spooned instant coffee into a mug.

Karina watched him from under lowered eyelids. He'd easily made himself at home. Did that come from living and working in so many different locations? Would he fit in anywhere? Or was it because this was the nearest to his own home he had? If so, did that indicate he might change his mind about selling?

That would mean having him in the house more often. Could she remain impervious to him then? Would she be able to turn away when her mouth cried out to be kissed? When the heat spreading down her body demanded physical release?

She doubted it. So he had to sell to her.

She eyeballed the man causing these problems. 'Would you give your share of this place to me as a loan? I'd get proper papers drawn up and make regular payments into your account.'

Did she have to sound like she was begging? Yeah, she did—because she was.

Logan straddled a chair and studied her. Probably trying to go from Mickey's pee-pee problem to could he lend her a few hundred thousand dollars within minutes.

Huffing out the breath she'd been holding, she started again. 'Of course I don't know your circumstances, but if you don't need the funds you'd get from selling, then it makes sense for you to lend it to me. A win-win answer.'

'When did you come up with this idea?'

Heat crept into her cheeks. 'Just now.'

'So you haven't thought it through?'

'What's there to think about? A loan with you is no different to a loan with the bank. I'd pay the going interest rate.'

That gorgeous mouth she'd kissed last night actually softened into a small smile as he kept on watching her. 'Why did the bank turn you down?'

'None of your business.'

Except it was if she wanted to borrow from him. 'Sorry, I take that back. I think the manager didn't like me, or he has a thing against lending to women. I have a small nest egg that I try not to touch except in dire emergencies.' She'd managed to save some of her wages before she'd moved in with Mickey. A deep breath in. 'But the account I use for day-to-day expenses is kind of empty.'

'Explain "empty".' That smile hadn't disappeared. Yet.

'My wages from the medical centre go in every fortnight and by the time the next pay day comes round I've used most of it. If not all of it.'

'What about the weekly amount from James and Maria's estate to cover Mickey's expenses?'

'The lawyers told me I'd have to wait for that until probate had been finalised.'

'That was done a month ago.' Logan's eyebrows rose in a disconcerting fashion and his mouth flattened with annoyance. 'You weren't told that?'

'I thought the lawyers would phone, or at least send a letter about it. It's hard. I don't want to seem to be waiting for James and Maria's money. It's not like Mickey's going without anything. The lawyers might think I'm a greedy cow if I ask.'

She'd made a vow never, ever to ask for money again and that meant from anybody. Unless it was a loan.

'Why am I not surprised at that answer?' The annoyance vanished and Logan's mouth widened into a heart-stopping smile, astonishing her.

'You think I'm a push-over, don't you?'

'You're a dedicated, big-hearted, caring woman who puts everyone before herself. Nothing wrong with that. But you also have to be practical. James would be angry if he knew you weren't getting the funds available.'

Did he have to sound so reasonable?

'It's not about whether you think you can manage. James can't be here for Mickey, but he made damned sure he could provide for him in the advent of a disaster happening—as it did.'

'I hadn't thought of it like that.'

'I'll get on to the lawyers today.'

His tone told her that those lawyers were going to wish they'd been paying her for weeks.

'Thanks.'

This conversation hadn't resolved the house sale issue, but she knew when to stop pushing. There were still more than three weeks to come up with a solution.

Standing up, she placed her mug in the sink. 'Time I got ready for the day.'

Logan stood up too. His knuckles under her chin tipped her head back, so she had to look directly at him. 'About me lending you the money...? I didn't say no. Or yes. But if I do agree I won't be asking you to pay me any interest.'

Her mouth fell open. Not a pretty sight. 'But—'

His thumb slid across her jaw. 'We're supposed

to be waiting a month before discussing what's happening with this place, remember?'

Sucker punch me, why don't you?

'You're right. I made that request. I guess I'd better stick to it.'

'One other thing, Karina. Have you thought about what you'll do when you meet someone you want to marry? Would you expect him to fall in with your plan to live here for the foreseeable future?'

'Me? Get married again?' She pulled away from that tender thumb to gape at the man. 'That *so* is not going to happen.'

'Come on. You can't know that. What if you meet someone tomorrow and fall in love? You're telling me you won't want to get married again? Or at least have a live-in relationship with him?'

Disbelief glittered out at her.

'That's exactly what I'm saying.'

'Your marriage break-up must have been horrendous for you to still feel like that.'

He stood watching her. Seeing what?

'It broke my heart.' *And it made me think hard about myself.*

'I guess that's not easily forgiven or forgotten.'

'No, but I don't blame him for everything. I let him control my life just as my father had conditioned me to do.'

Genuine kindness showed in Logan's eyes, causing a small lump in her throat that she had to clear before continuing.

'I come from money; went to the best schools, became a fashion icon, had the society wedding. All for nothing.'

Now Logan looked confused. 'So why are you trying to raise money from the bank to buy me out?'

'I walked away from it all.'

As his mouth opened with what was probably another question she held her hand up to stop him.

'What Ian did was wrong. But there was a silver lining in a convoluted way. I'd trained as a nurse but never got to put it into practice. I'd had my fun, but then it was time to fit in with the family line and become the perfect wife and hostess. My sister revels in all that.'

'You never did?'

'That's why I can't hold it against anyone. I always complied, but the day I learned of Ian's duplicity I learned there was more to me. A part I'd never explored. The person I wanted to become. And here I am.'

'I'm more than impressed. It must've taken a lot of guts. But that's no surprise. You've got that in spades.'

Her head jerked back a notch. 'Thank you.'

His simple yet empowering statement went a long way to reminding her that, yes, she *was* strong—could do whatever she had to for Mickey. Which meant fighting this man to keep Mickey's home.

Ironic, really.

'I'm glad you told me. It helps—'

'Kar—ina, I peed in my bed.'

She winced. 'Nothing like a dose of reality to get the day moving.'

'Go have your shower. I'll take care of this.'

Logan headed for Mickey's room, not pausing to see if she agreed.

She couldn't fault him, really. Except for one thing. He liked being in charge, too. Then again… Her fingers touched her lips where he'd kissed her last night. He was nothing like her ex at all.

CHAPTER SEVEN

'I DON'T WANT to use the potty.' Mickey stamped his foot on the bathroom floor.

Karina ached to pick him up for a cuddle, but that wouldn't help get the urine sample she needed to send to the lab. 'I need you to.'

There was a knock on the door and Logan asked, 'Can I help?'

'Yes.' Maybe Mickey would listen to him. 'I've got a problem.'

'So I heard.'

Logan's smile lightened the tension in her tummy.

'Along with everyone else in the street.' He hunkered down to Mickey's level. 'Hey, buddy, I want you to do your pee-pee in the potty this time so I can get it tested. If I don't do that then we can't make you better. Understand?'

'But I'm big.'

'Yeah, I know. But sometimes even big boys have to do this.'

'What about you?' Mickey eyed him suspiciously.

'Yeah, if I had to.'

'I don't want Karina watching.'

Phew. Progress. 'I'm out of here. See you over at the medical centre in ten. Mickey, Mr Grumpy's taking you to kindy. Be good for him, please.'

'What's that lad yelling about this morning? Doesn't he know he's got a quiet button?' Jonty stood on the back porch with his car keys dangling from his fingers.

Karina grinned. 'Good luck with that. Logan's getting him sorted.'

'You all right? You've got black puffy bits under your eyes.'

'Charming.' She'd applied more layers of makeup than sensible this morning, and obviously they hadn't hidden a thing. 'Bit of a sleepless night.'

'I saw the lights on during the night. Everything all right?' he asked.

Telling him about Logan's nightmares wasn't an option, but… 'You've got a rollaway bed in your back bedroom, haven't you?' She'd seen it when she'd been over at his house one time.

'Want it?'

'Can I borrow it for a few weeks?'

'I can only sleep in one bed at a time.'

'Thanks, you're a treasure. I'll get Leeann to help me carry it over at lunchtime.' She wasn't having Jonty lift it. He'd argue, but sometimes he had to remember he was eighty-two.

'Tell Logan to do it. He might need fattening up, but he's a man under those fancy shirts he wears.' Jonty stomped down the steps. 'Going to give those ruddy hens a talking-to. Only got six eggs this morning. Stupid females.'

That was why she loved Mr Grumpy. She never knew what was going to come out of his mouth next, but it would always be entertaining.

'I'll sort the bed.'

No way would she ask Logan to get it. He'd want to know why and then he'd refuse, saying it was totally unnecessary. But now she'd got the idea of setting a bed up for him in the lounge, she wasn't backing off. Next time he had a nightmare and wanted to sit by the fire he'd be able to lie down and hopefully fall asleep. He'd argue, but if the bed was in place and made up, then there was nothing he could do except ignore it. Which, when she thought about it, was exactly what he'd do.

'Can't say I don't try.'

Ice cracked under her shoes as she carried the washing basket to the line. She tipped her head back and the clear blue sky made her smile. It was going to be a cracker of a day, even if she was wearing thermals and thick tights.

By the time she'd hung the washing Mickey was calling from the porch. 'Can I knock on the washing?'

She felt the first towel she'd hung up. 'It's not hard yet. Give it a bit longer.'

'Here I come! Watch me, Karina.'

Mickey loved it when the washing froze solid on the line. And, honestly, she'd been excited the first time it had happened. They didn't have frosts like that in Auckland. Maria had laughed at her for getting so excited, calling her a big kid.

Maria. 'I miss you,' she said out loud. 'If only you were here to help me sort out what I'll do if Logan gets his way with the house.'

But then if she were here, the problem wouldn't exist.

Air caught in her chest as Mickey slid towards her. She whispered to Maria, 'Your boy is growing taller every day. You'd be so proud of him.'

She smudged an errant tear off her cheek, and probably wrecked her make-up.

'Knock-knock, who's there?' she asked Mickey.

'Jack Frost,' he answered as his little knuckles tapped a towel, then a pillowcase. 'He hasn't done it right.'

Karina laughed despite her sadness. 'Give him a chance. The washing's only been hanging a few minutes.'

'What's so fascinating about the washing?' Logan asked as he approached, looking heart-stoppingly gorgeous in a blue-and-white checked shirt and the navy jersey he must have bought when he'd arrived back in the country.

Should she tell him that the price tag and garment label were hanging down his back? Nah, not yet.

'This isn't any old washing, is it, Mickey?'

In a rush of words Mickey explained about the knock-knock game, and looked disappointed when he couldn't demonstrate what he meant.

'Come on, Uncle Logan. I want to break some ice.' He ran towards a frozen puddle.

Karina watched him and a big sigh puffed across her lips. 'I love that boy so much it scares me.'

Logan took her elbow and turned her in the other direction. 'I know. It's apparent in everything you do with him. He's very lucky he's got you.'

'He'd have been luckier still if he hadn't needed me. Or you.' *Sniff. God, don't cry now—not when Logan's right beside you.*

'Hard, isn't it?' His fingertips pressed gently into the crease of her elbow. 'You're surrounded by memories of Maria. What's good for Mickey isn't easy for you.'

Did he have to be so accurate? How the hell was she supposed not to cry now?

By sucking it up, breathing deeply and concentrating on that crack in the path until this moment of self-pity faded. That was how. She shouldn't be feeling sorry for herself. She was alive and well, and she had Mickey to care for. And she was tough. Or getting there, anyway.

Logan murmured, 'You're allowed to have down days.'

'Sure.'

But why today? Why now, when she'd just been laughing with Mickey? Why this moment, when Logan knew exactly what was going on?

He was too damned kind and understanding, despite his determination to do things his way. He was getting to her. In ways she'd never expected any man to reach her again. He was reminding her that her body was capable of loving a man, of being loved back. Unfortunately it couldn't be Logan who'd break through her barricades. He was on a mission. And while it included her, that was only to make sure his nephew's life ran smoothly. And his.

Tugging her elbow free, she stepped away, putting space between them while avoiding his all-seeing gaze. Somehow she managed to dredge up a smile that gave away nothing of what she really felt.

'You're supposed to cut the labels off a jersey before you wear it.'

Leaning towards her, he ran a finger along her jaw, making her gasp as shivers ran through her.

'Can I trust you with the scissors when we get inside?'

Wiggling a splayed hand back and forth, she said, 'You won't know until I'm done.'

Then she all but ran for the surgery, determined to get away from that vexing finger that had sent heat to her core, melted her in ways she'd never melted for any man before. Not even Ian.

The waiting room was overflowing with patients.

'Seems we've got an epidemic on our hands,' she said.

'The phone hasn't stopped ringing since I unlocked the door,' Leeann told them. 'The stomach bug's responsible for about a quarter of today's appointments, and the flu's doing the rounds.'

Karina groaned as she delved into one of Leeann's drawers for scissors. 'Fingers crossed none of us catch any of these things.'

Leeann said, 'I take it David's not coming in today?'

Logan answered her. 'I told him to stay home. He's over the worst and just needs to get around to eating again, but no point in him rushing back. I'm happy to work another day, and then he's got the weekend to fully recover.'

Another day working with Logan. That wasn't

so good for her equilibrium. This attraction she felt for him tended to trip her up.

Deal with it. Be professional. It's only for one more day.

Yeah, and then they'd go home together, eat dinner with Mickey and watch TV until bedtime. Very cosy.

The end of the month couldn't come fast enough, so she could get him out of her system and on his way. If only she didn't need to delay the situation about the house. Which reminded her...

'I've got to make some phone calls.'

Karina headed to her room and began dialling. She'd try all the banks before considering fishnet stockings, a minuscule black leather skirt and a walk along the wharf after dinner.

With two appointments arranged for early next week she headed out to the waiting room.

'Robyn Jenkins? Come through.'

Robyn was instantly on her feet and following Karina to the nurse's room. 'Thanks for putting me first. I'm going to be late for school as it is.'

'How's William? I'd intended ringing to see if he could come and play last weekend, but something always cropped up.'

Robyn's son William and Mickey went to the same kindergarten and loved playing together.

Robyn shook her head, then groaned.

'What's up?'

'Nothing. A bit of a headache.'

Karina studied the thirty-nine-year-old as she took a seat. Robyn was here for her regular blood pressure check-up. 'Where's this headache?'

'Behind my left eye.' Robyn rolled up her sleeve, ready to have her blood pressure read. 'Is Mickey enjoying kindy?'

'I think so.'

I don't want to go to kindy.

'William can't stop talking about Ben.'

'Ben?' Karina asked.

'The new boy,' Robyn explained. 'He joined a few weeks ago and William seems very taken with him.'

Maybe that explained Mickey's not wanting to go to kindergarten. William had a new friend and Mickey felt left out. It was inevitable, Karina supposed. William was highly intelligent for a young boy, whereas Mickey had learning difficulties.

The relief at finding a possible reason for Mickey's angst about kindy was enormous.

'Right, Robyn, how long have you had this headache?'

'Since before I left home.'

'What about your eyesight? Any blurriness? Double vision?'

Robyn started looking worried. 'Funny you ask that. I had to keep blinking to see properly as I parked the car. I'm not seeing too straight now either. The headache's getting worse. Like *bad*.'

Karina didn't want to panic Robyn. 'Stay there. I won't be a moment.'

At Logan's door she knocked.

'You're needed urgently.'

Logan joined her immediately. 'What's up?'

Quickly filling him in, she asked, 'Could it be a brain aneurysm?'

'It's possible. What's her history?'

'High blood pressure treated with statins. I'll read her BP now.'

Logan strode into her room, crossing immediately to Robyn. 'I'm Logan, standing in for David. Karina tells me you've got a sudden, sharp headache and double vision. Anything else out of the ordinary?'

He didn't muck about.

Karina wrapped the cuff around Robyn's arm and felt her trembling.

'I feel a bit sleepy.' Robyn blinked again and again.

Logan asked, 'Have you been taking aspirin in the last day or two?'

'No.'

'Any other drugs apart from your statins?'

'No.'

'I'm going to examine your eyes.' Logan looked around for an ophthalmoscope, opened the drawer Karina indicated. 'Try to hold as still as possible. The light can be annoying, I'm sorry.'

'BP's high.' Karina wrote down the figures and showed him.

Pulling out a chair, Logan sat opposite a now very distressed Robyn. 'I don't want you to panic but you're going to hospital.' He looked briefly to Karina. 'Can you call an ambulance? Stat one.'

As Karina picked up the phone and punched triple one, Logan returned his attention to his patient, acting and sounding like the complete professional he was, showing no signs of urgency when he must be desperate to have Robyn on her way to hospital.

'The sudden sharp headache, double vision and what I see in your eyes suggests to me that you might be having a small bleed on the brain.'

The last of the colour in Robyn's face drained away. 'Am I going to die?'

'You've come in very early on, which is good. In hospital they'll do a CT scan and some blood clotting tests to find out if it is a bleed or not.'

Logan spoke slowly and softly, pausing after each sentence for Robyn to ask questions, but she appeared too busy digesting what was happening.

After organising the ambulance Karina said, 'Robyn, do you want me to ring Tony so he can go with you?'

'Please. And the school won't know where I am either. I should be there by now.' Tears spilled down Robyn's face.

'I'll call them. I won't say anything other than you're too unwell to attend today. Tony can keep them posted.'

Out in Reception Karina told Leeann what was happening before asking, 'Can I borrow you to help me shift a bed at lunchtime?'

'No problem.'

Going into the doctor's consulting room, she

found Luke Browning—still waiting for Logan to finish his check-up. 'Won't be too long now, Luke.'

'No worries. I've got all morning.'

'How are those babies? Still waking you and Liz for feeds throughout the night?'

Luke and his wife had finally had triplets after their third IVF treatment, and they had to be the most loved babies on the planet. Karina had lots of cuddles with them whenever they came in for check-ups, and every time she wondered if she was wrong to think she could stay single and not have children of her own. But she loved Mickey as though he were hers. So what was her problem?

The sound of a siren cut off any further conversation. Karina met the paramedics at the back door and took them directly to her room, where Logan gave them the rundown while she helped Robyn onto the stretcher.

'Take care.'

Minutes later the medical centre returned to calm, and Logan picked up from where he'd been interrupted, but it was well after midday before they caught up with their patient list. Fortunately it was mostly a day of flu and tummy bugs and drug prescriptions and nothing else eventful.

Karina felt drained of energy and it was barely lunchtime. Getting up to Mickey so often had caught up with her.

Logan paused in the doorway to Karina's domain at the surgery. Sitting at her desk, hunched over a file, she looked tiny. With her big heart and exuberant personality he sometimes forgot how small she was. Even in his less-than-fit state it would be easy to scoop her up into his arms and hold her against his chest, kissing her senseless before exploring every inch of skin on that to-die-for body. After he'd carried her to his bed, of course.

Bed. With Karina curled into him.

Bed. *Duh...* That was why he was here. 'Why did I just see a bed being taken across our lawn and into the house?'

The stunned look on her sweet face told him she hadn't known he was there.

'What?'

Then that cute pink filtered into her cheeks. Embarrassed? Or guilty?

'Who was carrying it?'

'Mr Grumpy and a wheelbarrow.'

She leapt out of her chair. 'That man needs telling off. I told him not to do it. It's too heavy for him.'

'I don't believe it. You told Jonty not to do something? Talk about challenging him. He was always going to do it from the moment you opened your mouth.' He grinned at her mortification.

Her pearly whites showed between her lips as she sucked in a breath. 'Guess my brain was in sleep mode.'

Sleep… Bed… *Go, damn it*. His brain was fixed on sex—with Karina.

'You haven't answered the question. There are more than enough beds in our house. Why another one?'

The pink shade darkened to a rosy red. Those teeth dug into her bottom lip so hard it must hurt.

'It's going in the lounge.'

That drove away all thought of sex. 'You're setting up a bed for me to sleep on in front of the fire?' Like *that* was going to happen. Damn her for interfering. These were his nightmares, his problem. Not Karina's.

'Yes.'

Defiance glared out at him from under those long eyelashes to which she'd applied a load of mascara.

'Don't bother making it up. I won't use it.' If he lay down there he'd have a nightmare just as surely as he would back in the bedroom.

Tidying the files into a neat pile, Karina pushed out from the desk and stood. 'Lunchtime. Do you want soup and toast?'

Even as she asked she was heading out of the room.

Following her, he shook his head at her back view. 'You're avoiding the subject.'

'Not at all. But we've only got half an hour before we need to be back here. I can't sit around talking all day.'

'Why do you do this? Switch off when the conversation isn't going your way?'

It was like trying to discuss the house with her—impossible. When Karina made her mind up about something there was no getting through to her that there might be another solution. One that suited both of them.

Of course she didn't bother answering his last question.

As he reached the back porch Jonty was just leaving. His face was pale and he was yawning.

'Are you all right?' Logan asked. Had that bed weighed too much for the stubborn old man?

'Of course I am.' Jonty shuffled down the steps and began to stomp away.

'Jonty, there's a stomach bug doing the rounds. If you're feeling ill it would pay to have a check-up in case you've caught it.'

'Don't need no doctor. When you get to my age all they do is find too many things wrong with you and try to make you eat rabbit food and drink nothing but water.'

Logan stepped back onto the path. 'Come with me to the surgery while everyone's at lunch.'

'This thing that's laying everyone low... It's a twenty-four-hour bug?'

'Yes, with another day thrown in to get over it.'

'Then I ain't got that.' Jonty turned towards the gate that led to his house.

Oh, no, you don't.

'Let's go. I'll just take your temp, and I promise not to tell Karina to put your food through a blender before serving it.'

'Huh. That girl will do whatever she chooses,

whether you or I like it or not.' But he changed direction, now aiming for the surgery.

Jonty wasn't getting any argument from him about Karina.

In the consulting room he said, 'Right, park your backside on that chair. Do you feel nauseous?' When Jonty dipped his head in acknowledgment, he continued. 'Any fever? Sweats? Day or night?'

'Some.' Jonty turned his hat over and over in his gnarled hands.

He's afraid. He thinks he's got something serious and doesn't want to know. At his age who can blame him?

'What else?' Logan lounged on the end of the desk, as if he had all the time in the world to listen to this old guy.

'My gut hurts lots and the toilet stuff's not so good.'

'Any blood in your stools?' When Jonty raised an eyebrow in question he gave a more basic term for stools, then asked, 'Is it black?'

'A bit.'

'Up on the bed now and I'll check your stomach.'

Jonty stared at him, that hat almost spinning

now. 'I don't want you finding anything I can't deal with. You understand?'

'I do. Completely. But let me put it this way— what if you've got something easily treatable?'

'What are my chances? I'm too old these days.'

Logan put up a smile. 'You're also fit and very alert.'

Faded green eyes met his gaze and finally Jonty said, 'Thanks, lad.' He clambered onto the bed. 'Don't take too long. I've got to pick up those pipes so we can fix the drive in the morning.'

Logan warmed his hands under hot water, mulling over Jonty's symptoms and which tests to order. Those tests would be the hardest to obtain. Jonty would fight him all the way. But he had an ace up his sleeve. Karina. Jonty's Achilles' Heel. He adored her as much as she did him. He might grizzle about it, but they'd get those tests done if she told him to.

Listening to Jonty as he listed his symptoms of stomach pain, dark stools, weight loss and tiredness, Logan began considering Crohn's disease.

'Ever have any mouth ulcers?'

'One or two.'

'Right…' Now he knew which boxes to tick on the lab form.

* * *

It was late afternoon when Karina tracked him down in the tea room, getting a coffee. 'Mickey's very quiet since he got back from kindy. I hope he's not sickening for something.'

The boy was sitting in the corner, colouring in a picture of an elephant, and his desultory manner underlined Karina's comment. Still…

'Stop worrying. If he's crook we'll know soon enough. There's one plus. His urinary frequency seems to have stopped.'

'How can I not worry? Tell me that, Logan.'

He didn't get a chance.

Leeann strode into the room, saying to Karina, 'Becca phoned and said to remind you it's Friday night.'

'I'll call her back and tell her no.' Karina looked despondent.

'What does Friday night have in store?'

'Drinks at the pub. But I'm too tired to be bothered today.'

'Well, I'm not. It sounds like the best idea in ages. We've had a big day, so let's go unwind for a bit. Who normally looks after Mickey when you go out? Jonty?'

She looked stunned and she dipped her head.

'Come on, Karina.' He dropped an arm over her shoulders, squeezed her gently against him. 'It will be good to have some adult time.'

Leeann hadn't finished. 'Becca also said, Karina, that you should bring the doctor everyone's talking about.'

Logan laughed. 'There you go. I'm officially invited.'

'Wait till I see Becca,' Karina snapped as her face coloured a beautiful shade of red. 'I'm going to kill her. Slowly. Painfully.'

'You sure know how to make me feel wanted.' Logan dropped his arm and picked up his coffee. 'Just as well I've got a thick skin.'

'He's yummy!' Becca leaned close to Karina the instant Logan stood up to go for another round of drinks. 'No wonder you didn't want to bring him along for the rest of us to get to know him.'

'I didn't want to bring him because I have him in my face twenty-four-seven as it is.' She winced at her own unfairness. 'I just wanted some time to think without him there, to not think about anything except having some fun.'

'You're not seriously telling me you don't have fun with the yummy doctor?' Becca laughed. 'Come on, Karina, you're not made of ice.'

Her face flushed. 'Unfortunately.'

'Aha, so you *are* interested in him?' Her friend looked too darned delighted with that.

'Here you go, ladies.' Logan placed replenished beers in front of them and took his seat next to Karina. This time he managed to place the length of his leg against hers.

On her other side she got one of Becca's elbows in her ribs. 'Nice...'

'Shut up,' Karina whispered back, and adjusted her chair to put space between her and Logan. Picking up her drink, she tried to focus on the crowd and who was there that she knew.

Logan leaned closer. 'You any good at pool?'

'I know one end of a cue from the other.'

'She'll beat the pants off you,' Becca's brother informed him.

'Let's give it a whirl.' Logan stood and reached down for her hand. 'I haven't played for a while, but I bet I can beat you.'

'Now, there's a challenge.' Tugging her hand free of his, and feeling the instant cool where his fingers had been, she strode across to the table and began setting it up.

'Heads or tails?' He stood beside her, flicking a coin up and down in his right hand.

'Heads.'

The coin slapped onto the back of his hand. 'Heads it is.'

Karina chose a cue and went to the end of the table. Bending over to line up with the triangle of balls, she mentally crossed her fingers that she wouldn't make too much of an idiot of herself, then aimed the cue ball to break up the triangle. She could play, and sometimes she even won, but a champion she was not. As her first shot showed.

Hard as she tried, she couldn't ignore Logan when he nudged her aside.

'Let me show you how it's done, girl.'

Rolling her eyes, she laughed. 'You don't have a problem with self-belief, do you?'

'I'll have you know I beat the Nigerian health centre staff every time.' He winked. 'The fact we used sticks for cues and apples for balls had nothing to do with it.'

He sank three balls before missing a difficult shot.

'What did you use for a table?' Lining up her

next ball, she leaned over the edge of the table for better access. The resounding *thunk* as the ball hit the side of the pocket and dropped in made her chuckle. 'Take that.' *Thunk.* 'And that—and that.'

'A tin table with hats nailed to each corner.'

Laughter bubbled up just as she moved her cue. It slewed sideways and she missed her target. 'Look what you made me do.'

'Excuses, excuses. Again, let me show you how it's done.'

'Smarty-pants,' she coughed out around her laughter.

Then she got an eyeful of neat, butt-filled pants as he leaned so far over the table it was a wonder his feet remained on the floor. The laughter dried up; as did her mouth. *Oh, my.* Now, there was a sight for sore eyes. Any eyes.

'Looks like the drinks are on you.'

Logan's voice penetrated the heat haze in her brain.

'Why?' A glance at the table gave her the answer. 'The best of three?'

She began emptying the pockets and putting the balls back into the wooden triangle.

'You're on. But first I need my beer. It's hot work, playing nice to a lady.'

'That was nice? Distracting me and then sneaking balls into pockets when I wasn't looking?'

Don't ask me where my gaze was.

'All part of the plan. Win by means foul or fair.' He brought their beers across. 'Get that inside you and see if it doesn't improve your eyesight.'

Did he know how he'd distracted her? He couldn't. He'd been facing the other way. He wouldn't have known she'd been interested in his derrière. She studied him over the rim of her beer bottle. He looked decidedly cocky. Maybe he'd planned it all along. Well, two could play that game.

'Your break.' She nodded to the table and waited impatiently as he broke the triangle, then went on to pocket five balls.

'See if you can beat that.' He grinned as he straightened up.

Quickly averting her gaze from his backside, she grinned back. As she'd decided: two could play that game.

Studying the balls on the table, she found the one she wanted to drop first and walked along to the side, where she leaned as far across as possible without losing her balance. *Thunk.*

Her opponent was silent, and she didn't dare look around to see if she'd distracted him as neatly as he had her.

Finding another suitable ball to aim for, she once again arranged herself over the table and sank it. When all the balls were gone she turned to him, smoothing down the top that had somehow ridden above the waist of her trousers, and said airily, 'We're equal.'

He blinked and shook his head. 'You think?'

Oh, I know.

But she kept those words to herself.

CHAPTER EIGHT

'ANOTHER PERFECTLY CLEAR DAY.' Karina stretched her arms above her head as she peeked out of the window on Saturday morning.

Logan's mouth dried as her breasts were pushed higher. When she bent at her waist, leaning first to the right and then the left, her arms still high, she looked so lithe he wanted to grab her and slide his hands over each and every tempting curve, from those breasts down to her bottom.

That bottom had grabbed his attention last night as she'd sprawled across the pool table to reach a ball. He'd been blindsided by the curvy vision that had totally distracted him and lost him the second and third game.

She straightened and faced him. 'Did you go back to sleep after your hot chocolate?'

Talk about a passion-killer. Another nightmare had brought her to his room at three in the morning. He'd have been happy to have her waking him for pleasure, but not to drag him out of hell. *Be grateful she did.*

'No. And before you ask, I didn't use that bed.' When he saw a question forming on her lips he held a hand up. 'Sleep's highly overrated.'

Instantly he wished back his thoughtless retort. Hurt blinked out at him from those chocolate eyes. In trying to deflect her questions he'd upset her.

'I'm sorry. That was uncalled for. Can I ask you not to talk about my nightmares if I promise to stop coming out with half-baked comments like that?'

The hurt faded and a half-smile touched her mouth. 'Sure. I'm not really a nosy person, but I do like to help where I can.'

'Unfortunately you can't fix me.'

Though he wished she could. But for that to happen he'd have to tell her about the PTSD and watch any respect slide out of her eyes. It shocked him how much he never wanted to lose that.

Changing the subject before she could ask why she couldn't fix him, he said, 'Did Mickey sleep through?'

'Not a peep. I wonder what the other night was about?'

'Just one of those things. I'm glad the results came back negative for an infection.' Seemed Mickey was over that episode. 'What do you do on the weekends?'

'I coach Mickey's football team, but we've got a bye today.' She sipped her steaming tea. 'Hey, why don't we go up to the Mount Arthur car park? Mickey hasn't seen snow.'

From Africa to Mount Arthur? From forty-plus degrees to something barely above zero? Different. But didn't he want different? There weren't likely to be any guerrillas hiding in the trees there.

'How are your snowman-building skills?'

'Non-existent. But I've got carrots and bananas in the pantry.'

'What for?'

'The nose and mouth.' She gave him that impish smile. 'Whatever else were you thinking?'

He hadn't been thinking. That was the problem.

'Shall we see if Jonty wants to join us? We were going to finish the drive today, but he might like this better.'

'I'd forgotten about that. It's a great idea. He might forget worrying about his health for a while.'

'He *is* worrying, isn't he? Not that he'll ever admit it. Do you think he'll go to those appointments at Nelson Hospital that I've arranged? He was very unhappy about them. Should I offer to drive him over next week?'

It wasn't as though he'd be working, and he might be able to call in at the reclamation yard for a window frame to replace the existing one in the laundry that dry rot had wrecked.

'I reckon he'd go with you. He told me you remind him a lot of James, and they were close.' Karina touched his forearm with those orange-tipped fingers. '*Were* you two alike?'

'You mean you haven't worked that out yet?' He smiled to lighten the question, in case she was still wary of him. She could change attitude quickly.

'You're more stubborn than James. Far less likely to change your mind once you've made it up.' That elfin face turned cheeky. 'And James would never have dug up that driveway, or considered painting the house. That's manual work, and he hated getting down and dirty.'

'True... Strange, when both our parents are hands-on kind of people.'

'They absolutely love living on Stewart Island, don't they?' Karina shivered.

Warmth snuck in under his ribs. 'Yep. It's about as remote as you can get, unless you go to the Chathams. The weather's extreme, the fishing's amazing, and they don't ever want to leave.'

'Have you visited?'

'Often.'

He drained his mug and went to rinse it under the tap. 'What time do you want to head away?'

'Ten? The roads won't be quite so icy then.'

'We'll take the four-wheel drive. It's a lot safer on the terrain we're going to, even if you do have new tyres on your car.'

Karina pulled a face. 'Where would I be without Jonty?'

'I'll go and ask him what he wants to do.'

'I haven't seen him out and about yet. If he's not in our yard he's usually in his shed.'

'You're not thinking something's happened to him?'

He felt a twist of worry for the old guy. Already Jonty had made an impact on him, had him caring. That was the problem with staying too long with people.

'I'm probably overreacting.'

'On my way.' Logan opened the back door and reached for his boots.

A shot rang out. He dropped to the porch floor, rolled sideways and looked around the yard. Where had that come from? Who was out there? His gut tightened as his ears strained for any sound, his eyes scoping the yard.

'Stop. Go away, you bastards.'

'Logan? What are you doing? Are you all right?' Karina loomed over him.

'Get down!' As the order slid across his tongue he heard a motor, then a car speeding down the road, backfiring repeatedly. Expletives formed but with a herculean effort he managed to keep silent.

'Logan? Talk to me. You're freaking me out.' Karina crouched beside him. 'What happened? Did you slip?'

His chest rose as he filled his lungs. *One, two, three, four.* It would be easier to lie. 'I thought I heard a gunshot,' he muttered. Truth was hard, but he had to try it.

'You've been shot at? In Africa?'

Those eyes were filled with disbelief. Or was that shock?

He nodded and sat up. The porch was freezing. Quickly getting to his feet, he picked up the boots he'd dropped. 'Yeah, Nigeria is a fun place to work—believe me.' Shoving one foot into a boot, he tugged at the laces and tied a knot.

'Were you ever hit? Shot, I mean?' The question was quiet, and filled with loads more questions.

'No.' Logan straightened and looked directly at Karina. 'No.'

That wasn't a lie. A dead hostage was no use to anyone. The guns had been pointed a metre either side of him, their bullets kicking up the dust close enough that he'd felt the grit on his legs, the warning explicit. *Don't think you can get away.*

Logan looked deep into Karina's eyes, saw nothing but her big-hearted concern and felt his heart roll.

'But you had a bad time?'

'Yeah, Karina, I did.'

Then he bent and brushed his lips over hers to stop her talking. Except the instant his mouth touched hers he had to have more, had to lose himself in her. His arms came up and wrapped around her, hauling her warm, compliant body close against his chilled, frightened one. He could forget the horror while Karina deflected it.

He deepened his kiss. Karina returned it, meeting each of his moves with one of her own. Then her arms slid around his neck and pulled him even closer, and he felt safe. Warm and cared about and safe.

'Good morning, you two. Hope you've given Mickey his breakfast?'

Karina jerked out of his arms and spun around to stare at Mr Grumpy as though she'd never seen him before. Her fingers were pressing her bottom lip as if she was trying to keep that kiss there.

'Mickey?' she squeaked.

'Is having a lie-in.' Logan stood behind her, his hand on her shoulder, and eyeballed Jonty, who had a stupid grin on that wrinkled face of his.

'You won't be interested in doing any more digging this morning, then.' Jonty clomped up the steps to stand right in front of them.

Logan relaxed. 'I was on my way to see you.'

'Humph,' Jonty grunted.

Ignoring the interruption, Logan continued, 'We're heading up Mount Arthur—taking Mickey to see the snow. Do you want to come?'

'Why the heck people like rolling around in that stuff is beyond me.'

'Come on, Jonty. It will be fun. Can you picture Mickey throwing snowballs?' Karina had finally found her voice.

'Unfortunately, I can. What time you leaving?'

Karina gave him a quick hug. 'Ten o'clock. I'll pack a lunch and some drinks.'

Jonty stomped back down to the path. 'None of that lemonade stuff for me. Hot tea is the only thing.'

'Guess that's a yes, then?' Karina called after him, and then turned back to Logan.

Her face was his favourite colour—pink. Her eyes were filled with mischief and wonder. Then she leaned close and traced her finger over his chest.

'I'm sorry you had a bad time. Let's have some fun today.'

He just had. What could be more fun than kissing a hot woman? He hadn't enjoyed himself so much in a long time. Which showed how much he'd lost his grip on reality.

He had no right to be kissing his nephew's guardian. It would only set up difficulties for further down the track. What if they disagreed on Mickey's education or health plan? How could they resolve things amicably if they'd briefly got too close and personal? How did parents deal with these situations? *Parents.* He was not nor ever likely to be a parent, given his penchant for working in inhospitable places. He was a guardian. Full-stop. But that meant giving the same love and care and concern, didn't it? Like a parent.

Logan swore silently. He was caught whichever way he looked at it. Sighing, he gave up his one-sided argument. 'Want me to get Mickey up? Give him the good news?'

'Sure. There are plenty of thick clothes on the bottom shelf of his closet.'

Karina turned to go inside.

Who'd have believed something as ordinary as a car driving by could have led to him kissing her? Though he was glad she'd stopped pushing for more answers than he was prepared to give, he felt they'd crossed a line in their relationship. No longer were they only Mickey's guardians at loggerheads about where he'd live. Those problems remained, but now Karina knew a little of what drove him and he knew how far she was prepared to go to look out for those she cared about—a very long way.

He did not need or want that from her. The things that had tipped his world upside down, including James's death, were his to absorb and cope with alone.

Karina sat up front with Logan, giving him occasional directions as they drove through the valley alongside the Motueka River. Frost glittered on the grass in the paddocks and on kiwi fruit vines while the sun made a feeble attempt to warm the world.

She tried to ignore that kiss. Failed. If only that kiss had a future. But it had come out of a moment of shock on her part and fear on Logan's. His fear had been quickly followed by embarrassment, and then he'd kissed her. To erase that fear? Or in the hope of diverting her so she'd forget what she'd seen?

'What's snow?' Mickey shouted from behind her.

'It's like ice, only all mashed up. Like if I put it in the blender to whizz round and round.'

Logan flicked an amused glance her way. 'Where do you get these ideas?'

'Have you got a better way of explaining it?' Her smile was teasing, taunting him to come up with something.

Which he damned well did. Too easily. 'It's like hard ice cream, buddy, but it doesn't taste half as good.'

'Yippee! I'm going to have ice cream all day!' Mickey yelled.

'Shh, you're giving my eardrums a hard time.' Karina looked around and shook her head at the excited wee guy. 'Mr Grumpy's probably wishing he'd stayed home right about now.'

'No, he isn't. He's having fun with me.' The decibels dropped infinitesimally.

Jonty winced and rubbed his ears. 'What did you say? I've gone deaf.'

Mickey knew a cue when he got one. He yelled, 'You and me are having fun!'

'Mickey,' Logan growled in a low tone. 'Stop shouting. There's no need for it.'

'I like yelling.'

'Stop right now. It's not nice.'

'Okay.' That was said with much less energy.

Karina let go the breath she'd been holding. 'Phew,' she whispered. 'Thought we were in for an argument.'

'Who makes the snow?' Mickey asked next, without deafening anyone.

Logan shot her a grin. 'Answer that one.'

She pulled a face at him and launched into an explanation. 'It's part of the weather. You know how rain comes out of the clouds? Well, snow is like frozen clouds that land on the ground, but it's thicker than rain.'

'Very good,' Logan muttered.

'Can I jump and splash in it?'

'You can jump in it, and you'll get wet, but it won't splash. It's good for making snowmen. We're going to build one today.'

'Can I build my own?' The yelling was back.

'Quieter, buddy. And yes, you can. Mr Grumpy's brought along a sled for you to ride down the slope on, too.' Logan turned up the mountain road Karina pointed to. 'Here we go.'

Karina immediately asked, 'Isn't riding a sled dangerous?'

'What's the worst that can happen? He'll tip over, for sure, but you said there aren't any cliffs, and the slope's not steep. It's good for him to push his boundaries in a safe environment.'

This was why Mickey needed his Uncle Logan around. 'I suppose...'

Looking out at the snow-covered trees, Karina felt a small fizz of excitement in her veins. She hadn't done anything like this for so long.

Behind her, Jonty said to Mickey, 'It's going to be freezing cold and you'll soon be wet as a fish. The way those two up the front go on, anyone would think this is fun.'

Smiling, she glanced across at Logan and saw him smiling too. Impulsively she touched his arm, and spoke quietly enough that only he could hear. 'Knew he'd be thrilled to come.'

'Exactly.'

'It's rude to whisper in front of others.'

'Yes, Jonty.'

Finally Logan pulled the vehicle into a parking space and looked around. 'Appears half of Motueka's here.'

'Definitely the place to be.' There were children in every direction, and adults trying to keep up with their offspring. 'Let's get amongst it.'

Mickey ran straight for the biggest mound of

snow he could see and jumped into it. His look of astonishment when his feet disappeared was priceless. Karina clicked her camera madly, afraid to miss any of his antics.

'Come on. You're missing out on the fun.'

Logan reached for the camera but she ducked out of his reach and clicked a picture of him. Just for the record. Nothing to do with capturing that beautiful face and its rare happy expression. 'Go and jump in with Mickey. I'll get a couple more shots, then join you.'

'Silly fools. They'll get soaked.' Jonty stood beside her.

'That's why there's a bag of towels and clothes for everyone in the back of the car.' She snapped more photos—plenty of Logan as well as Mickey. It was a golden opportunity to take Logan's picture without having to explain why.

Jonty put out his hand. 'Give me that fandangled thing. I'll take the snaps while you join in the circus.'

'Okay. Do you know how to use it?'

'It's a camera, isn't it?' His gnarled hand closed around the small device. 'Which button do I push?' Five minutes later Jonty declared, 'I know what I'm doing, girl. Leave me to it, will you?'

The photos probably wouldn't be great, but what did it matter? She'd have memories of today, and she could take more pictures later on.

Bending down, she scooped up a handful of snow and shaped it into a ball. 'Hey, Mickey, look at this.' Taking careful aim, she lightly threw the ball at his middle.

Mickey whooped and shouted, 'I want to do that. I'm going to make the biggest.'

He made one so big that when he tried to throw it the ball landed on his feet.

'Here, buddy, make smaller ones so that you can throw them at Karina and make her laugh. Like this.'

She got pelted, with all three males ganging up on her. Jonty had given up being photographer to join in the fun, even laughing once when he got a direct hit from Mickey.

'I liked the sled best.' Mickey hung on to Karina and Logan's hands and swung between them two hours later, as they made their way back to the car park and a late lunch. A smile lit up his face, and his eyes were bulging with excitement.

'Even when you tipped over and got your head buried in the snow?' she asked. Her heart had stopped for a moment, but Mickey had come up laughing and demanding to fall off again.

'I tasted the snow. It's yucky. Not like ice cream at all. What's for lunch? I'm starving.'

'I've got bacon-and-egg pie.'

By the way all the faces lit up she knew she'd won some points. She wouldn't mention the cream doughnuts she'd bought from the bakery until Mickey had eaten his pie, otherwise he'd go straight to the second course. She was spoiling him—spoiling them all, really—but what the heck? In these chilly conditions people needed food in their tummies, and why not have something naughty but tasty?

Though if Logan was right, and Jonty had Crohn's, then he needed to be warned that he shouldn't eat too much of that sort of food. *Damn*, she should have thought about that and brought something more suitable.

'Watch out!'

The shout came from behind them.

Logan snatched Mickey and leapt sideways in one smooth move. She jumped after them. A young boy on a snowboard shot past. Looking around for Jonty, she saw he was further over, well out of danger. Shuddering, she muttered, 'Idiot. He shouldn't be doing that in a crowded area.'

'I think he might've lost control further up and doesn't know how to stop.' Logan held Mickey in his arms as they watched the boy finally crash to a stop in a large snowdrift. 'He seems to have survived unscathed.'

A loud voice indicated that the boy was getting a telling-off from his father. Karina grimaced. 'Parenting never stops.'

'A lifetime commitment,' Logan said, then asked, 'Where's that lunch? I'm in need of a hot drink, too.'

She heard the shiver in his voice. 'Guess this is a shock to your body?'

'You're not wrong there. But, hey, I'm enjoying it.' He grinned at Mickey, who was still in his arms. 'What about you, Mickey? Isn't this awesome fun?'

'Yip. My nose is cold.'

The food went down fast as everyone was ravenous. But standing around devouring pie and doughnuts had them feeling the cold too much.

'Do we head home now or have some more games in the snow?' Karina wondered aloud.

'I want to ride on the sled again.' Of course Mickey would fight the going home suggestion.

Logan placed the sled on the snow. 'Come on. I'll pull you to the top.'

Karina trudged along beside them. 'You're going to sleep well tonight, my boy.'

At the top they turned the sled around and Mickey clambered on, standing up on his feet. 'I'm going to do the same as him.' He pointed to an older boy on a snowboard.

'No, Mickey. Sit down.'

Too late.

The sled was already moving down the slope and Mickey was struggling to keep his balance. Logan leapt after him, jogging alongside the sled, ready to catch him if he slipped.

Swallowing the worry tightening her tummy, Karina walked down behind them, watching like a mother hen over every move Mickey made.

Things were going perfectly until the sled

bounced over the end of a ski as its owner hur-
tled across in front of Mickey. The sled slid sideways fast, tossing Mickey into the air.

'Mickey!' she screamed, and ran, each step
sinking into the snow.

'Kar—ina.' He rolled over in the snow and stared
around. 'Kar—ina!' he yelled.

She and Logan reached him at the same moment
and dropped to their knees at his side. Logan put a
hand on his chest, his fingers making quick work
of checking him over.

'You're all right, buddy. Just a wee cut on your
chin.'

'I don't want a cut. It hurts.' He rubbed his chin,
and when his fingers came away red he shrieked.

Karina reached for him, bundled his little body
up in a hug. 'Shh, sweetheart. It's all right. You
just had a little crash.'

You're never going to ride a sled again.

Mickey cuddled in tight, crying and hiccupping
against her chest. 'I was going good like that boy.'

Logan collected the sled and laid it beside them.
'You were doing great, buddy. It takes practice to
be perfect.'

'I don't want to do it now.'

Logan pulled a small ball of twine out of his pocket. 'Fair enough, but how about you sit on the sled and I'll tie this rope to the end so I can keep you from going too fast?'

Mickey shook his head. 'I might fall off again.'

'Not if I've got hold of you.'

Karina stood up, Mickey still in her arms. 'It's—'

'Give it a go, Mickey.' Logan cut her off. 'If you don't like it we'll stop.'

Wriggle, wriggle. Mickey wanted to get down. She locked eyes with Logan as she lowered the boy, shook her head at him.

'Back on the horse,' he said quietly. 'He'll be fine.'

I worry far too much. Yeah, she got it. But mothers, even surrogate ones, were allowed to.

Of course it was an uneventful trip back to the car park, where Jonty stood, stomping his feet and muttering about silly people who didn't know when they'd had enough fun for one day. He took the sled and headed for the four-wheel drive.

Logan lifted Mickey to hold him in one arm, took Karina's hand with his free one and said,

'Let's head home. I think we've all had enough excitement.'

She didn't pull her hand free. It felt so right to be close to him after the day they'd shared. Later on she'd probably regret this, but now she wanted to be a part of someone.

'Hey…' Logan stopped a few metres short of his vehicle and turned to face her. 'You're one hell of a woman.'

Then those lips she was getting to know and enjoy captured her mouth again. His tongue slipped inside and she tasted him.

All too soon he pulled away. 'Come on. Jonty will be keeping score if we're not careful.'

CHAPTER NINE

By the end of the next week Karina had two bank loans on offer to consider, and a driveway that no longer flooded in a downpour. That had been proved already, when the frosts had moved over for a weather bomb that had brought more rain than anyone had seen in years. She also had a vase of colourful winter roses on the dining table from Logan and Mickey, for giving them such a fun day out on the snow.

The arrival of the beautiful flowers at the surgery had had Leeann staring in amazement and Karina's stomach fluttering like a butterfly in the breeze. Ian had used to have his secretary send her flowers every Friday afternoon, but those elaborate floral displays had never warmed her soul. Nothing like these, with their handwritten note from Logan.

On her way out of what had used to be her bank for the last time, having closed all her accounts and transferred her funds to the new bank she'd finally chosen, she saw Becca.

'I can't believe Logan's been here nearly two weeks already.'

'And...?'

Karina's heart sank. What could she say? Kisses didn't count as world-changing events, and nor did the numerous hours she'd wasted thinking about Logan. It seemed Logan didn't know when to back off out of her head space.

She cut Becca off at the pass. 'And nothing.'

'He came to Friday night drinks.'

'He wanted a break from everything.' *Don't ask what 'everything' involves.*

'He had a great time playing pool with you.' Becca grinned wickedly. 'He hardly took his eyes off you. If I wasn't the generous-hearted woman I am I could've been insulted.'

Unfortunately for her friend, Karina didn't want to talk about the man who was haunted by something so terrible he relived it almost nightly in his sleep.

'Look, he's here for Mickey and they're getting on so well. It's "Uncle Logan this...", "Uncle Logan that..."' Mickey would be heartbroken when Logan left, but that was out of her hands. 'And Logan's offered to give David a break by working mornings all next week.'

'That's kind, but do you like him? Think he's sexy?'

'A bit.' She'd never been able to lie. 'All right— a lot. He's caring and giving, and a lot sexy. But he's leaving in little more than two weeks, so I can't afford to play around with him.'

As long as it's not too late and I haven't already caught the Logan bug.

Because he'd sneaked into her heart a little bit while she'd been busy making him hot chocolate. She cared about him and for him, and at the moment that was survivable. She would miss him when he left, but her heart would be intact.

Really?

Of course. Absolutely of course.

Becca watched her far too closely. 'Bringing him along for drinks again tonight?'

'Drinks? Is it Friday already?' She slapped her head. 'How could I forget?'

'This Logan's seriously distracting you.'

'He could look after Mickey while I join you.

That's why he's here—to bond with his nephew, not to go out with me.'

His eyes were sometimes filled with laughter and happiness and at other times were bleak and desperate, but whenever he was with Mickey his expression was always bright. She wouldn't think about that deep, hot look he wore around her.

A text message hit her phone. Digging deep in her bag, it took her a moment to find the phone amongst all the junk that somehow seemed to accumulate when she wasn't looking.

Are you coming home for lunch? We're missing you. Logan.

'Got to go. Seems my men need me.'

Becca had the nerve to laugh. 'You're hooked! Your men? That's brilliant.'

Karina opened her mouth to refute it, but snapped her lips shut. How could she explain that whatever affected Mickey affected her? Make that whoever had anything to do with her boy touched her. Nothing to do with her heart and Logan.

Tell that to the birds.

Saying, 'I'll text you about tonight,' she left her friend, still laughing, and headed for the car to go to the supermarket. On the way she replied to Logan.

Why's Mickey at home? He should still be at kindergarten.

Logan came back instantly.

The teacher called, said he was upset.

Why does my boy suddenly hate kindy when he's always loved it? Is Logan playing the 'Uncle' card too hard? I should never have let him stay home that first day. She laughed softly. *Listen to me, sounding like a mum—a mum in all but DNA. Cool.*

When she let herself into the house thirty minutes later she found Logan and Mickey lying on the rollout bed in front of the fire. Her feet turned to lead even while her throat ached with emotion. Mickey's small body was curled in against Logan, his cute face pale and his eyes closed. Logan's arm was wrapped around his nephew's body, holding him close, protecting him. They looked perfect together.

Slashing at the tears on her cheeks, she crossed to stand beside the bed. Whatever Mickey was unhappy about, she'd never forget this picture. He belonged in Logan's arms.

When she opened her mouth Logan raised a finger to his lips. 'Shh. He's only just fallen asleep,' he whispered.

Nodding, she quietly asked, 'Want anything? A drink? Lunch?'

'A cup of tea wouldn't go amiss. And a sandwich.'

He looked so hopeful she wanted to laugh.

'You eat like a horse, yet it doesn't stick to you. If I ate half what you do I'd be enormous.' She squinted at him. 'Actually, your face has lost some of that gauntness.'

'So I'm gaunt? Charming.'

Glancing at Mickey, she felt the fun go out of her. 'He's obviously tired, which isn't normal.'

Logan winced. 'He's peed a lot this morning, so I've collected another specimen to send off.'

She shivered, forgot to whisper. 'You don't think this is the start of something worse? An underlying illness?'

Panic flared, rapidly drying her mouth, cranking up her heart-rate and crunching her stomach.

'Karina, take a deep breath and listen to me.'
He no longer whispered either.

His calmness had her instantly taking that breath.
'I know I worry too much, but I can't help it.'

'Despite the urinary frequency and tummy
aches, I don't believe he's ill. He's tired, but think
of the energy he's been expending in the snow and
helping me and Jonty with the digging. There's
plenty of colour in his face. Nor is there too much,'
he added, when her mouth opened to ask exactly
that.

Forcing the panic down, she acknowledged that
Logan was more qualified medically than she'd
ever be. If he wasn't overly worried maybe she
shouldn't be either. 'Is it because he's getting close
to you and will do anything to stay home with
you?'

A rueful smile told her he knew the problems
that he would cause when he left. 'Sorry, but I
admit I'm enjoying being with him.'

Good. And bad. Another person in Mickey's
life who would leave.

'I'll get that tea.'

'And a sandwich?'

Placing the steaming mug and a plate stacked

high with ham sandwiches on a stool within easy reach of Logan a few minutes later, she told him, 'I'm due back at work. Anything else I can do before I go?'

Shaking his head, he whispered, 'I've got it covered.'

'I'll pop over when I'm not busy.' Then she couldn't help herself. 'You're really bonding with the wee man.'

'Not quite how I thought it would go down.'

The look of love he gave Mickey grabbed at her heart.

'You must be doing it right if he's relaxed enough to go to sleep with you.'

Usually if there was even a hint of distress the only person Mickey had wanted since he'd lost his parents was her. But that had been changing over the time Logan had been here. She should feel a twang of jealousy that he was so comfortable with Logan, but all she knew was relief. Things were looking up as far as this relationship was concerned.

Mickey and Logan were playing Snakes and Ladders when she got home. The dinner she'd prepared earlier was heating in the oven, and Jonty was watching the news.

Karina sighed. 'That's what I call domestic.'

Logan raised his head and locked eyes with her. 'Are we going out for Friday night drinks?'

'I guess…' Honestly, she'd prefer to stay home and keep an eye on Mickey.

'Jonty's prepared to look after our boy.'

Our boy? That sounded as if they had a family thing going. 'How's Mickey now?'

'I don't want you to go out,' Mickey answered her. 'My tummy's sore. And my head—'

Logan cut in. 'Haven't you spent the last thirty minutes complaining because you're starving and don't want to wait for dinner? Not to mention being a gymnast on the couch?'

'Stay home with me.'

'No. Karina and I are going out and you will be good for Mr Grumpy. Do you understand?'

'Yes, Uncle Logan. But—'

'Dinner's ready!'

Karina cut him off and hurried to dish up for him and Jonty. She and Logan would eat when they returned.

But Logan changed that.

'Is there a Thai restaurant around here?' he asked as they finished their beers.

'Just along the road,' Karina informed him. 'It's really good, what's more.'

'I'm drooling at the thought of a hot red curry. Want to have a meal there?'

'I'd love it, but what about Mickey?'

'I'll ring Jonty and see if he's okay to stay on for a bit.' He held his hand up in a stop sign. 'I won't be asking if Mickey's well. Jonty's raised his own kids. He'll know if there's anything we should be worrying about.'

'Okay.' She forced herself to relax by breathing deep yoga breaths, dragging the air all the way down to her tummy, where it mixed with the beer and sent bubbles up her throat. *Great.*

Becca did her usual elbow-nudge thing. 'You're going on a date! How long's it been?'

'For ever,' she answered without thought. *Wait up.* 'It's not a date. We're both hungry, so we're doing something about it.'

'The food warming in your oven at home would do that,' Becca pointed out.

'I guess...' It was a date. *Oh, my God.* 'I don't do dating.'

'You do now. And you couldn't have picked a sexier guy if you'd checked out every male in Motueka.' Becca grinned. 'No, I'm not interested. He's too brainy for me.'

Logan snapped his phone shut. 'Sorted—let's go.'

Becca wrapped her arm around Karina in a hug and whispered, 'I want every detail.'

'This satay is superb.' Nearly an hour later, Karina licked her lips of every last dot of sauce. Becca was going to be annoyed when she told her that. And about the delicious entrée of crumbed squid rings and spring rolls. 'How's that curry?'

'Heaven.'

She'd figured it might be, since he hadn't said a word since his first mouthful.

'And the wine's not bad either. Hope you're up to walking home, because driving's out.'

Logan topped up their glasses from the bottle he'd ordered.

'Two weeks ago I stomped home in a right snot on three-inch heels—tonight's not going to be a problem.' She had on her favourite boots. 'Not a drop of rain in sight either.'

'No puddle-jumping, then?'

'You spoilt that when you fixed the drains.' She smiled to take any perceived sting out of her words, then changed the subject. 'Where did you do your training?'

'I followed James to Christchurch, which is just up the road from Ashburton, where we grew up. I had some half-baked idea that we could flat together, become best buddies and all that. Didn't factor in that he already shared a flat with five other guys. But I soon teamed up with some other students and had a blast.'

'There's something about getting away from home. It changes you for ever.'

Except her father had insisted she return to the fold the moment she had her nursing qualification in her hot little hand and she'd complied. How different would her life have been if she hadn't?

Logan started telling her about some of the pranks he'd got up to as a student. The wine ran out so they walked home, still talking about themselves.

For Karina, the best part was having Logan's arm around her shoulders, holding her close to him. Her arm around his waist soaked up every movement, and had her dreaming of her bare arm against his skin. Her blood sizzled with desire.

I'm on a date. Yeah, and very shortly I'm going to be home, tending to Mickey and cleaning up the kitchen after Jonty. Hey, Cinderella, where's the pumpkin?

Their date came to a jarring end the moment they walked in the door. Mickey and Jonty were arguing over who'd cheated at Snakes and Ladders. Was that even possible?

Karina shook her head and lifted Mickey up into her arms. 'Bedtime for you.' Tears streaked his sweet face and shadows underlined his innocent eyes.

'Don't want to go to bed,' came the inevitable reply.

'Want and get are two different things.'

He was exhausted. Overtired, as it turned out. Sleep did not come easily, so that by the time he did finally succumb more than an hour had passed and all the heat that had fired her body had buttoned off. Not that it would take much to fire it up again.

In the lounge, Logan and Jonty were talking about the rugby game on TV. Deflated further, she turned away, headed for the kitchen and the mess on the bench.

So much for a hot date. She'd overreacted to the intimacy of sharing a meal and being held close to Logan on the walk home. Of course he wasn't interested in anything that might make life difficult between them when they dealt with the house, the surgery and Mickey's future.

Angry at herself for even considering that they might have an interlude that was about them and nothing else, she banged pots and plates into the sink and turned the tap on so hard water drenched the front of her top.

Logan stirred the pumpkin soup he'd found in the freezer and checked the oven temperature. He'd found heat-and-eat buns right next to the container of soup. Everything was all set for when Karina came in from the surgery for lunch, which should be any minute now if they closed on time. It being Saturday, and theirs the only surgery open today, they might be overrun with patients.

He was getting a kick out of doing things with and for Karina. Like last night at the Thai restaurant. They'd been so relaxed together it had been marvellous: sharing those entrées and watching her perfect teeth bite into the spring roll he offered her. He'd been turned on all the way through the meal.

But that was nothing compared to the tension tightening his muscles as they'd walked home. *All* his muscles, which hadn't made for comfortable walking. It would have been all too easy to stop and kiss her senseless. Hell, he'd wanted to kiss her right from the moment they'd left the house, heading for the pub. Her perfume had filled his vehicle, teasing and taunting. Her hands moving in the air as she'd chattered non-stop had had him aching to feel them on his skin.

With every step he'd wanted to stop and wrap Karina in his arms while he devoured her with kisses. But a little voice at the back of his head had prevailed. What if Karina took him too seriously? Thought they might have a future? Believed he'd change all his plans and stay on here with her?

Even then he'd been unbelievably close to giving in to temptation. Then they'd walked in the front door and had been confronted with the chaos that was Mickey.

Mickey hadn't wanted anything to do with anyone except Karina, which had left him out of the loop, so he'd joined Jonty in the lounge. In hindsight that had been a good thing, because it had given him time to cool down and realise what taking Karina to bed would have done to their relationship. He wasn't prepared to make a mess of that just because he desperately wanted her. Not when he had to negotiate a truce on what to do with the house and the surgery.

The back door opened and a blast of cold air smacked into the kitchen, bringing him fully alert.

'Something smells delicious.' Karina skipped into the kitchen.

'I've been raiding your freezer.' When her eyebrows rose he added, 'Soup's the only thing on a cold day.'

'I was hoping for something warm.'

Warm? You're hot.

As she looked around, worry creased Karina's brow. 'Where's Mickey?'

'In the lounge, making a chart to keep score of who wins the most Snakes and Ladders games.'

While Karina went to see him Logan opened

the oven and placed the buns on the rack. 'Five minutes until lunch is ready,' he called after her.

'Mickey says he's hungry. Again.' She smiled from the doorway, where she stood with their boy in her arms.

'Hope you don't mind, but I also got out a beef casserole to thaw for dinner. I haven't had anything like that since I was last at Mum's, and the moment I saw the container my stomach started doing a loop-the-loop.'

He began ladling soup into bowls.

'Go for it. Does this mean I'm not on dinner duty tonight?'

She sat Mickey on a chair and lifted his hair off his forehead, her hand automatically stopping to feel his temperature. She had all the instinctive parenting skills necessary, though she should relax a bit.

'I'm a genius at heating pre-cooked meals.'

Her smile widened, then slowed. 'Some of Jonty's tests have come back. Looks like you're on the right track—though the faecal occult blood result isn't back. His white count's slightly elevated, with a predominance of neutrophils, including band forms.'

'That'll be because of the numerous mouth ulcers. What about his B12 and folic acid? Iron?' Logan placed a bowl in front of Mickey. 'Blow on it first. It's hot.'

'Iron borderline normal. B12 and folate low.' Karina picked up one of the remaining bowls and settled at the table. 'Funny how I didn't notice he was losing weight until you said something.'

'You often don't when you're around someone all the time. Eventually it would have dawned on you. He says he's lost seven kilos since Easter.'

'Did he say why he's been taking so much aspirin?'

'Headaches, stomach pain, sore knees. The aspirin could've exacerbated the stomach problem and given him ulcers there too.'

Flicking the hot buns onto a plate, Logan placed them on the table and sat opposite Karina. This was cosy. A man could get used to it.

'Careful, Mickey.' Karina pushed his bowl closer to him.

'How do you think Jonty will cope with a strict diet regime?' With Crohn's disease some foods were definitely off the menu, and Jonty would have to work out which were the trigger food groups peculiar to him.

'He's not called Mr Grumpy for nothing.'

'True.'

The soup was delicious and required total concentration.

'From the way that's going down, I'm guessing it's also been a while since you had soup.'

When he raised his head he found Karina watching him with questions in her eyes. 'I'd forgotten how tasty something as simple as pumpkin soup can be.' Had he deflected those questions? What did she want to know this time?

He soon found out.

Karina licked her spoon until it shone, then asked, 'Are you looking forward to going back to Africa?'

He shivered. 'Yes.'

'I'm getting mixed messages.'

Too damn observant. That was what she was. *Come on. Think of something to say that won't reveal the truth but isn't a lie. Come on*, he repeated in his skull.

'I'm happy to go back. There's so much to do there. It's never-ending.' As her brow furrowed he knew she wasn't buying into his explanation. 'I haven't been in NZ long and I still need to unwind completely.'

He also needed to be here. Mickey was getting used to him, wanted him in his life. That had to be good, but it also complicated everything.

The furrows remained in place. 'Will you go to the same base as last time?'

Try as hard as he might, he couldn't prevent the shudder that rocked him, and she saw it, those eyes widening ever so slightly.

'No,' he muttered, and pushed off his chair to get more soup in an attempt to shut her up without growling at her. Offending her was not on his agenda. He liked her too much. Besides, they had to get along for Mickey's sake. 'I'll probably go to Uganda next time, even though I haven't quite finished my last contract.'

'Will it be another twelve-month stint?'

'They usually are.' He had yet to discuss his deployment with his boss. Hopefully by then he'd be able to say with full confidence that he'd got over the kidnapping.

She stood beside him, holding out her bowl for more. 'That's not exactly what I asked.'

He knew that. His shoulders rose and fell as he ladled soup into her bowl.

Back at the table Karina eyed him as he sat down. 'I know I'm a pest, but I have to look ahead. Knowing if you'll be coming home to see Mickey during the next year will make it easier to tell him what to look forward to.'

Her honesty could be a pain, but he couldn't fault her reasoning. 'It wouldn't be fair to leave you on your own with Mickey longer than a year.'

Even that was too long to expect Karina to hold the fort. But twelve months back in that stinking heat, wondering where the next attack might come from, fearing being taken and locked up again, wasn't going to be a picnic either.

'I'm quite happy with the situation, but it worries me that it's not always easy to contact you. What if something goes wrong? Like Mickey getting seriously ill and my needing you?'

Nurses and doctors were known to look for all sorts of illnesses when it came to their own kids, and there was no denying that, to Karina, Mickey was her own. But…

'Mickey's doing great. I suspect the headaches and tummy aches are about attention-seeking.'

As she tapped her bottom lip repeatedly with her spoon he wanted to hug her tight, kiss away those worries screwing up her eyes. He wanted to make everything easier for her.

'How would you feel if I was living here? Was available all the time? Would that make you feel I was infringing on what you're doing with Mickey?'

Now, where the hell had *that* come from? Next she'd be thinking he planned on staying around.

Her spoon clattered into her bowl and her chair tipped back as she raised startled eyes to meet his gaze. 'You're not serious?'

That hurt. 'What if I am? Mickey's as much my responsibility as yours. Besides, I'm not looking forward to leaving him for so long.'

So she didn't want him here, didn't want to share parenthood. She'd had it her own way too long.

'Sorry, that came out all wrong,' she backpedalled. 'It would be great for Mickey if you lived in Motueka.'

'But apparently not in the same house as the two of you?'

That hurt too. He'd become used to Karina being around all the time. He liked sharing meals and looking out for Mickey with her, and had enjoyed working alongside her in the surgery. Seemed she didn't think the same. Of course she was right. Sharing a house really wasn't wise. What if, despite her protestations, she did meet a man she wanted to settle down with? It was bound to happen one day. She was too attractive to remain single for ever. He'd be like a spare wheel around the place. *Come on...* He'd hate it—and he had no right to that emotion.

Karina might be sneaking under his radar and touching his heart, but he wasn't about to run with that. She'd already been hurt badly by her ex and she didn't need a basket case next time around. Nor did Mickey need the fallout a broken relationship would bring if it didn't work out between them.

Standing, he gathered up the empty soup bowls and took them to the sink. 'You're safe. I couldn't stay still in one place long enough to make a life for myself here.'

She didn't need to know that he'd begun to feel that this might be the place where he could let go of the fear and grab at the sense of belonging that sometimes caught him. Whether that was the location and its townsfolk, or just two people in particular, he still didn't know. But, as he didn't usually go looking for places to leave his heart, he suspected it was Karina and Mickey who'd weaved their magic around him, causing this disturbance to his head and his heart.

Karina couldn't get Logan's words out of her head.

'How would you feel if I was living here? Was available all the time?'

He had refuted them almost immediately, but it had been as though he was testing her: seeing what she felt about the idea.

Well, buster, the answers to those vexing questions are entirely up to you. She flicked the towel she was folding, getting a small satisfaction out of the snapping sound it made. *I can't tell you what to do with your life.*

Logan living here would be the best thing for Mickey and the worst for her—even if he lived in another house. Already she'd grown too close to him, and she wasn't looking forward to the day he left.

Male laughter reached her from the direction of the shed, where Logan and Jonty were sanding the frame on a set of windows they'd bought at the demolition yard in Nelson during the week.

Another maintenance job being attacked; another thing soon to be ticked off Logan's list. He seemed to be getting immense enjoyment out of doing these jobs, saying on more than one occasion that it was great seeing the results of his hard labour.

'What's hard about it?' Jonty had asked one time when they'd all been in the garden. 'It's what real men do.'

Logan had laughed at Jonty's poke, no doubt safe in the knowledge that the old man was more than happy to work alongside him.

You're all man—right down to the tips of your toes. She'd had to slam her mouth shut on the words.

Logan was comfortable showing his softer side. He spent hours with his nephew and had been more than happy to step up when needed in the surgery. Oh, and he had a chest and a butt that were definitely real man.

But she didn't know what to make of Logan's query about him staying around. She'd be absolutely thrilled, she suspected. He was impossible to ignore, despite her best intentions. He was knocking away at the barriers she'd hoisted around her heart. Often she found herself thinking about him at times when she had no right to be—times when she was meant to be reading patient notes or making sense of Mickey's erratic behaviour, which she hadn't been able to find an answer for even by searching the net.

Logan. Get out of my head. Now. Stay away.

See? She didn't want him moving here permanently.

Yeah, I might, though.

What if she was falling in love with him?

Then he's got to go. No argument.

He mightn't be anything like power-hungry, control freak Ian, but she'd loved Ian with all her being and she suspected that was how she'd love Logan if she allowed him into her heart.

That was how she loved Mickey.

That was how she loved. Full-stop.

With a child, that was okay. Parents loved unconditionally and took the knocks along the way.

But to love a man like that again, knowing full well how painful it would be at the end, would be utterly foolish. She wasn't ever again going down that black hole. And the only way she could be sure of that was by not getting involved with Logan.

Logan might be wonderful with Mickey, but he also liked to be in charge, liked controlling everything around him. Such as selling the house. In his book he was right: no argument. Just like her ex and her father. She was never again going to be that person who did as others bade in the hope that they'd love her more.

No, siree. I know how this unfolds. I give in once, the second time is easier, and so it goes.

Love Logan or not, she wasn't getting involved with him.

CHAPTER TEN

A SHOUT WOKE Karina from a deep sleep.

'Here we go again...'

She rolled out of bed and groped for her robe and slippers as another cry ripped through the house.

'Logan?'

These nightmares weren't getting any less frequent.

In his bedroom, she went through the routine of shaking him awake and making him aware of where he was, and who with, before turning to head to the kitchen and the chocolate and milk.

'Don't go. Stay here with me for a bit.'

Logan's voice was raspy with sleep and whatever had disturbed him.

'It doesn't help, going to the lounge. The nightmares follow me.'

Sitting up, Logan shuffled sideways, making a space on the bed for her.

As he tapped the mattress beside his hip he added, 'I won't bite.'

He leaned back against a pillow, looking exhausted and nothing like a man who might have light entertainment on his mind. Karina's eyes followed his hands as they tugged the bedcovers further up his chest. He'd taken to sleeping in a tee shirt and shorts, but no clothing or bedcovers could blot out the image she already held of his body.

Easing down, she swung her legs up and stretched them alongside his—except hers barely reached past his knees. 'I'm nothing like my mum and sister. Too short and not thin enough.'

Logan stared at her unglamorous pyjama-clad pins and picked up her hand to fold his strong fingers around hers. 'You've got curves in all the right places, and for the record curves are not to be sneered at.'

He squeezed her hand.

'Thanks…I think.'

She felt the shivers still passing through him intermittently. *What were the nightmares about?* she asked herself for the hundredth time. It was the one question she'd never verbalise. The look in his eyes when he came awake after one was not something she wanted to be responsible for bringing back.

'I was kidnapped for ransom. In Nigeria. By guerrillas.'

Karina gasped, shocked at his disclosure and stunned that he'd read her mind. Squeezing his hand in return, she felt increasing shudders rock through him, and moved sideways so that her shoulder rubbed against his upper arm.

She finally managed a lame, 'Logan, that's absolutely terrible.' What could she say? 'Why did they take you?'

'Money. They came into our quarters in the middle of the night and took three of us at gunpoint. That's why I didn't make it home for the funeral. I had no idea James and Maria had died until after I was released.'

'Why didn't we hear about this in New Zealand? Surely it should've made headline news?' Reporters weren't known for their discretion. Not the ones she'd dealt with, anyway. 'Your parents don't know, do they?'

'No.' Logan shivered again. 'Because of my English passport my director didn't dispel the notion that I was British, so I guess the local media missed that a Kiwi had been taken. Secondly, I was mistaken for the son of an English lord who was working at a neighbouring camp. Only after the man had been sent out of the country under-cover were the guerrillas informed they held the wrong man.'

For someone who didn't ever talk about this he suddenly seemed incapable of stopping. Karina held his hand and waited, wondering if he even realised he was telling her this stuff.

'I got lucky,' he said angrily. 'Luck being rela-tive. Six weeks after we were captured I saved a child who'd fallen in the river we were camped by. Technically the lad had drowned, but I was able to revive him. Turned out he was the lead-er's only son. After a further two weeks of hang-ing out in a hut I was sent away with a man from a neighbouring village. At first I thought he was going to knock me off and leave me to the hye-nas, but after four days I began to hope. Hope's a strange thing. It grips you, teases, taunts, screws with your mind. We walked all night and most of the day, lying up under any tree we could find when the temperatures were unbearable. By day six I was getting so weak I doubted I'd make it to wherever we were headed, and then suddenly there was a small town on the horizon. After that everything was a blur until I found myself back at base.'

'Thank goodness.' Her thumb traced back and forth on the back of his hand. 'What about the other two? You said they took three of you.'

'Still in captivity, last I heard, but negotiations are underway with the US government.'

She shivered. *Unbelievable.* It was like something out of a movie: over-dramatised and unrealistic. Except this was true.

'Those scars on your body...?'

'The brutes enjoyed whipping us with the flat side of a machete. The slightest pressure either way and our skin would be sliced. Infections were rampant.'

Admiration for him ramped up, filled her heart. How did anyone come through all that and still be a kind, caring person like Logan was? Here he was, getting to know his nephew, working hard to improve the house for her—whether they sold it or stayed. Yet he said he would return to that area. *Crazy.* Why would he?

Turning, she saw wariness in his eyes as he watched her. Was he searching for disgust on her part because he felt he'd failed somehow? He'd be looking a long time.

Laying her head on his shoulder, she wanted to weep for him, but knew better. He'd hate that. She asked, 'How long after reaching your base did you leave Nigeria?'

'Three days. I was sent to hospital in California to be checked over and to talk to the shrinks.'

'Then you came home?' Did Motueka feel like home to him?

'Home... It's not a word I use often. I've always focused on being wherever I'm needed and not on putting down roots.'

Unbelievably sad. She'd had problems, but she had always known where she belonged. 'And now?' she asked softly.

'I haven't a clue. I still need to help people. That's in my psyche. But do I do that in Africa or Asia? Or right here in Motueka? I haven't a clue,' he repeated.

'Go easy on yourself. Sort those nightmares out first.' She leaned harder against him.

Logan wrapped his arms around her and brought

her even nearer. His chin nestled on her head. Strands of her hair lifted with each of his breaths, then floated back down onto her cheek.

This felt right. If she pressed her cheek hard against his chest she felt his ribs, and now she understood why they stood out as they did. He needed feeding up. Under her ear, his heart beat fast. Occasionally a shiver still shook him. Lifting her hand, she touched his chest, his chin, paused. Pulled back and snuggled close again.

They stayed like that, listening to the house creak as outside the night air cooled down towards freezing point. Then Logan moved carefully. His lips brushed her forehead, trailing feather-light kisses from one side to the other and then down her cheek to her chin and along her jawline. Over her throat, moving slowly downward to the V in her pyjama jacket, his breath so soft it caressed her.

Her breathing faltered around the lump of desire suddenly blocking her throat. Lifting her hands, she slid her fingers into his thick, dishevelled hair and massaged his skull with soft circles, holding him against her breasts.

Logan groaned and pulled away to tug her down

the bed until she was on her back. His fingers shook as he tried to deal with the buttons keeping her chest covered. 'Help me here,' he muttered through gritted teeth.

With a hand on his chest she pushed him away and sat up to shuck off her robe. About to attack the buttons on her top, she paused, drinking in the sight of Logan's chest as he hauled his tee shirt over his head.

'Karina?' The shirt landed on the floor. He was staring at her with such hunger in his eyes.

'Do you want to stop? Say so if you do.'

Her eyes tracked the outline of his ribs and moved over those muscles as she shook her head, not trusting her voice. To hell with the buttons. She jerked her top over her head and then lay back to lift her butt and slide her pyjama bottoms down past her thighs.

Logan returned to where he'd left off; kissing a trail between her breasts, moving to one breast to tease her until she thought she'd scream with need, only have her other breast put through the same tummy-tightening, heart-cranking sensations. Her muscles grew tighter and tighter. Her centre was wet.

Her hands flailed against the bed as she tried to reach for him. 'I have to touch you!' she cried.

'No. Not yet. One touch and I'll be gone. Let me give you this.'

'But I want to feel you. My skin on your skin.'

It was torture to lie there, being made love to without giving something back. She wanted Logan to feel what she was feeling, to share the sensations pouring through her, yet he didn't seem to think he was missing out.

'Your turn's coming. You'll get more than a handful, I promise.'

Again that beautiful mouth shifted its centre of attention, this time trailing more of those delicious kisses over her stomach before moving ever downward, until he reached the hot, molten apex at the top of her legs. Any thoughts about what she should be doing to Logan were lost as he went from kissing to licking and all too quickly drove her to the brink with a gripping need clawing through her.

Just when she knew she couldn't take any more without exploding into a thousand pieces, Karina moaned. 'I need you inside me.'

Logan hesitated. 'Do you have a...?'

Karina shook her head. 'It's okay. I have an IUD.' She'd had it fitted while she was married, as Ian hadn't wanted to start a family.

Logan rose above her to kneel between her legs, his reaction to her big and beautiful. She reached for him, slid her hands over, around his length. And cried out. *Beautiful.*

Logan lowered his body and pressed the head of his erection to her. Her hands stroked until he pushed inside, deep within her heat. As he filled her she nearly wept with joy and love. When he withdrew to drive inside again her breathing caught, her lungs stalled, her muscles quaked with need. Then her climax cracked, whipped through her, taking over and blotting out all thought, leaving only exquisite sensations rocking through her.

Slowly Karina's breathing came back to something like normal, as did her heart-rate. Logan lay sprawled half across her and she held him tight, making the most of this moment. His chest rose and fell rapidly. Sweat glistened on his back. She tugged at the bedcovers. In the chilly night air it wouldn't be long before they were cold, despite the heat between them.

She wanted to laugh and to cry, to be quiet and

to talk. She wanted to repeat what they'd just shared, yet was worried it might not be the same. She couldn't believe that making love after all this time could be so wonderful, that she'd been wrong to think she would never know a man again.

'Thank you,' she whispered.

'That should be my line,' he gave back, and carefully rolled over to pull her in against him, spooning them together, his arm wonderfully heavy on her waist, his hand splayed across a breast.

'We can share it.'

Her mouth was swollen and tender as she smiled into the semi-dark. Her fingers traced her lips. *I feel whole—like a part of me that I didn't know was missing has been given back.*

But she was wise enough to know that this night had not changed anything. She still intended staying on in this house. Mickey still needed her to fight for what he required. Logan hadn't emptied his skull of those demons plaguing him.

She might be feeling languid and filled with warmth right at this minute, but it was only an interval, brought on by a nightmare and her unexpected need to get close to Logan just once.

Her eyes drooped closed and she snuggled further into the warm body at her back. She'd enjoy the moment and stretch it out for as long as possible.

Logan held Karina like a delicate gift, never wanting to let her go. He didn't know if it was in his power to lift his arm and set her free. Not that she was trying to move away. Quite the opposite.

This was a precious time; an intimacy beyond making love. Their sweat-slicked bodies locked together as they cooled, their hearts slowing as that intense, mind-blocking release eased off. Of course he wanted to do it again, but not right at this moment. Now he wanted to treasure this amazing woman who'd shown the tormentors in his head where they could go—for a while at least.

'You sent them packing,' he murmured.

'I'm glad. Now we know there is a cure.'

He chuckled softly. As if it was going to be that easy. But he didn't even mind so much at the moment. Around Karina, anything seemed possible. Even slaying dragons would be doable.

'I've moved on from hot chocolate.'

'You can have both.'

She said nothing else for a while, and he began to think she'd fallen asleep. Then...

'You gave me back my heart.'

'Your ex bruised you that badly? He stole it and never returned it when he left?'

Was this the first time for her since her marriage had fallen apart?

'I thought I'd given him so much of myself there was nothing left for anyone else. Now I'm not so sure.'

Her voice had got lower and lower, and he strained to hear her clearly.

'Karina, like I said: you're a beautiful woman with a big heart.'

She'd done so much for him, right from the day he'd turned up here, full of ideas about what they should be doing with the house and the surgery. Despite their disagreement about the property she hadn't flinched at extending him a hand.

Under his arm she tensed.

'Karina?'

Silence.

'Hey, I didn't say that earlier just so I could have sex. I'm not saying it now because I'm grateful. I believe it. Truly believe it. Okay?'

Had her ex told her how lovely she was to get his own way? While all along he'd been bonking his other woman on the side?

'Okay.'

The tension relaxed and she wriggled against him, that perfect backside rubbing where it counted and causing him to bite down on the need springing to life and tightening his manhood again.

She stilled. Of course she'd have felt his reaction. Kind of hard to miss.

He grinned. He was probably crazy not to be acting on it—he would do so shortly—but holding Karina in his arms had to be the best thing to happen to him in a long time. He continued holding her, burying his face in her silky hair, breathing in her scent. Sex and sweat and woman. He'd be a millionaire if he knew how to bottle that. But he didn't want to share it. This was his moment; their moment.

Carefully pulling the covers up to their necks, he shifted to get more comfortable. There were still hours left to enjoy before they had to get out of bed. He should be shivering from the cold, but he was warm for the first time in months.

Sure, he'd been hot beyond comprehension out in the middle of Nigeria, but this warmth was inside him, heating the corners where he'd shoved his fear and vulnerability and cold anger. This warmth was all down to Karina.

He could get used to it. Which was why he wouldn't repeat it. There'd only be one night with Karina. It wouldn't be fair on either of them to continue being intimate for the remainder of his time in Motueka and then for him to walk away as though it didn't matter. Because it would. He'd have nudged aside one set of problems for another. But staying on permanently wouldn't work. He still had to face down his fears.

He shuddered. That day seemed to be racing at him and he was so not prepared. Despite tonight, and making love with Karina, the fact was those evil men did dominate his head, his life. He knew he had to prove they hadn't won, that he could banish them for ever.

He needed to get back to being normal. That wasn't going to happen while he was shut away in small-town New Zealand. No, that required a visit to what was for him enemy territory. Another shudder. Then and only then did he stand a chance of making a life for himself. Maybe even a life that included a family.

He already had Mickey. Karina would complete the picture.

But he was getting way ahead of himself. They'd made love once and here he was thinking too far ahead. Just because Karina had him beginning to feel whole again, it didn't mean she might contemplate a relationship with him. She'd made a niche for herself with Mickey, and she certainly didn't need a shell of a man living with them.

So he'd enjoy this moment. Holding Karina, feeling complete, even knowing it couldn't last, meant everything to him. She'd done so much for him in her kind and generous way.

Now he had to do something for her.

Unfortunately he knew exactly what that was.

CHAPTER ELEVEN

KARINA SANG UNDER her breath as she hopped out of the shower. Singing out loud would only bring complaints. But, damn she felt good this morning. Nothing like good sex—no, make that very good sex—with Logan to make the day wonderful.

It's six a.m. and the rain's bucketing down, and I'm on top of my world.

Uh-oh. Rain.

Where were the buckets?

Pushing into her robe, she dashed to the laundry and hastily placed buckets under the drips, took another to the bedroom next to Mickey's and placed it under the newest problem.

'When did that leak start?'

Logan leaned the shoulder she'd kissed so thoroughly during the night against the doorframe, his hands in his jeans pockets, feet crossed at his ankles, sexy stubble on his chin. He looked like a very tired movie star.

'Last night too much for you, lover-boy?' She flicked a finger under his chin. Heat sizzled through her veins as that stubble softly rasped her skin. Tingles licked the base of her spine.

He caught her finger to run his tongue over the tip. 'Are you avoiding my question?'

Her happiness slipped a notch. 'There was a damp patch on the carpet after the last rainfall.'

'I guess you'll be buying more buckets this week, then.' He didn't look so happy either. 'You should've told me.'

This was why they shouldn't have slept together.

'Let's make tea and toast. I'm hungry.' All that exercise had used up last night's dinner. She pushed past him. 'You must be, too.'

She'd noticed while exploring his body during the night—how could she not?—that his ribs didn't stick out quite so much as that first time she'd seen his chest.

Breakfast was quiet until Mickey woke up. When he protested loudly about wanting to stay home again her heart wasn't in trying to reason with him. Instead she picked him up, took him out to the car and buckled him into the seat; surprising herself as much as Mickey.

He yelled at her all the way to kindergarten, so by the time she got to the clinic she had a pounding headache to go with her darkening mood.

All morning Karina was aware of Logan's voice through the wall as he talked to his patients, and it reminded her of him talking dirty as they'd made love. Had sex. They had not made love. That would mean they were going somewhere with this, and anyone with half a brain only had to look into Logan's eyes and know the only place he was going was out of here and far away.

He was still haunted by what had happened and his way of clawing back some control in his life was to organise hers.

Voices intruded from outside. Workmen with ladders and tools were striding along the path.

'What the—?' Leaping up, she ran for the door and charged out onto the lawn. 'Excuse me. Who are you?'

One of them stopped and stared at her. 'Mrs Pascale?'

Not likely. 'Karina Brown. This is my property. What are you doing here?'

'Seems there's a mistake. I thought this was Dr Pascale's house?'

'It is.' The man himself came up behind Karina. 'I'm Logan Pascale. You're Harry?'

'That's me.' He jerked a thumb over his shoulder. 'This the roof you want looking at?'

Harry Whoever flicked his gaze back and forth between Karina and Logan.

'That's right.' Logan stepped around her. 'Come in and I'll show you where it's leaking. I'd like you to check the whole structure while you're at it, and give me a quote for both repairs and a full replacement.'

Karina seethed. 'Excuse me?'

'Be with you in a moment,' Logan called over his shoulder.

Oh, boy, you are so going to regret this.

She charged after him. 'What happened to talking to me about any repairs?'

'I didn't realise I had to run absolutely everything past you.'

'It should've been a reasonable assumption. I do live here. All the time. Unlike you. I have every right to know what's going on with my home. I also think it only fair if I have a say on the decisions being made.'

'I only talked to the roofing company this morning, and we have been rather busy in the clinic.'

Karina came close to stamping her foot. Close, but she didn't. 'You've obviously been thinking about it before this morning.' A picture of him leaning against that doorframe flashed into her head. 'You could've told me about this instead of giving me a hard time about buckets. Is this how I'll learn you've contacted a real estate company too? They'll just turn up with their listing pads in hand and go through my home as though they own it?'

'Cut it out. It's a huge step from roofing to selling.'

'So you're not getting the house ready to sell?'

Logan's eyes narrowed. 'We're having that discussion at the end of my stay, remember?'

'So it's fine for you to prepare the house for sale, but I'm not supposed to think about it or, heaven forbid, even mention what we might do?'

She'd come full circle—had swapped one control freak for another. And here she'd been thinking she'd made progress in the standing on her own two feet stakes. *Idiot.*

'Karina, breathe deep and calm down. We—'

The heel of her shoe was buried in the soft ground as she gave in to the urge to stamp her foot. '"Breathe deep", he says. Like it works for you. *Not*. Anyway, I don't want to calm down. I want to tell you exactly what I think.'

Those grey eyes became the colour of cold steel. 'I'm listening.'

'From the moment you arrived I've been hearing what you plan to do with Mickey's home and the clinic. Not once have you said, *Let's discuss our options*. Oh, no, you want the whole package wrapped and sealed so you can go away again with a clear conscience. You think that's the best thing for Mickey—and for me. Well, I'm telling you, buster, you are *wrong*. I am not moving. *Ever*. Nor is *my* boy.'

Anger and pain shot through those eyes and she knew she'd gone too far. Mickey was in his care too. Except she was the one who'd be here day in and day out, every month of the year and beyond.

'Finished?'

As if she'd trust that calm tone. 'I don't care if the roof leaks, or the carpet needs replacing. It doesn't matter if I have to juggle locums to keep the surgery running. This is my home. You can't sell it out from under me. Us, I mean.'

Hot tears ran down her heated cheeks but she didn't care. He could think what he liked about them as long as he got the damned message.

'Leave me alone. Leave us to live quietly and happily, as we were before you arrived. I don't need you interfering and telling me what to do.'

'You have to start facing reality.'

'Yours? Or mine?' she snapped.

He stood tall, staring down at her. Some of those lines around his mouth and eyes had filled out over the weeks he'd been here. *Huh?* Why was she thinking about that now? Then he got her full attention.

'I think it's a good idea if I move out for the rest of my stay in Motueka.' Light glinted off those steely eyes.

'I agree.'

But what scheme would he be cooking up when he had more time on his hands? Who would wake him from those nightmares? She opened her mouth to say that if he stayed they'd work something out. Stopped. Pressed her lips together. Maybe they wouldn't. It was too late. Putting everything off until the end of his stay had been a mistake.

'I'll come see Mickey every day.'

'Of course.' She didn't expect any less of him.

'I'll get my things at the end of the morning session.'

'Right.'

He spun away, turned back. 'I'll pick Mickey up from kindergarten today and take him with me until dinner time. Is that okay with you?'

'Yes.'

God, now they sounded like a divorcing couple, fighting over the kids.

'This might be for the best anyway. He's getting too close to you and his little heart is going to break when you go. Moving out of the house will soften that blow.'

For Mickey and for her.

Logan's cheeks paled. 'I get it. I've stayed too long. But he *is* my nephew. I *am* his family.'

The longing lacing his words stole into her heart, slowed her anger.

He reached a hand out and ran a finger over her chin. 'This isn't over, Karina.'

'I think it has to be.'

She should be grateful he was on the move, but she couldn't explain the way her heart thudded wildly as she watched him cross to the corner of the house and disappear around the back. He really was leaving, and taking something of her with him—a piece of her heart. At least it was a piece and not the whole package. It felt beyond hard to watch him go, but it would have been a lot worse in another week.

Toughen up. Take everything on the chin. Get back to life as you know it.

Quiet and happy. Lonely and boring. At least she'd know where she was. Or would she? Just because Logan was no longer staying here it didn't mean he wouldn't be hatching plans. Didn't mean she'd switch him off, out of her system. Impossible after last night, after knowing his body, knowing how he moved when he came inside her.

The sound of screeching tin had her turning her head in the direction of the roofers.

The house would feel empty, but at least it would be dry.

Logan swore as he tossed his few clothes into a holdall. What the hell had happened? One minute everything had been hunky-dory, the next he was out on his butt. Not that he could blame Karina for that. He'd put his hand up—said he was going. But she'd been quick to jump down his throat with all her unfounded accusations.

Now he had to find a motel room that was far enough from humanity that no one would hear him calling out in his sleep. Not everyone would be as patient and understanding as Karina. No one would care like she did. He'd gone two nights without a nightmare this week. A first. All down to Karina.

Outside, he went to talk with Harry, agreed on a price for a new roof, and walked down the drive to his vehicle, refusing to look back. Somewhere behind him Karina would be nursing a patient or making a sandwich or drinking tea. What she wouldn't be doing was wishing he'd stay.

Karina, I've fallen in love with you, somewhere between your puddle-jumping antics and last night, when I held your naked body tight against mine. Leaving is breaking me, but staying will break you. I'm not the right man to love you. You need someone willing to face his demons like you've done: bravely and without fanfare.

So he had things to do for her, to get the show on the road. Chucking his bag onto the back seat, he climbed into the vehicle and scrolled down the contacts list on his phone.

'Uncle Logan, have you come to get me?' His favourite little man ran at him an hour later. 'Pick me up.'

Logan obliged. 'Want to go for a ride to Nelson?'

Mickey's yells of excitement brought his teacher racing outside. 'What's going on? Is Mickey all right?'

'He's fine, Scarlett. I'm taking him out of kindergarten early today.'

'He's been missing a lot of kindy since you came on the scene.' Scarlett shrugged. 'You do a lot with him. He adores you.'

'The feelings are reciprocated.'

But give it another week and the boy might hate him. He squeezed Mickey tighter, breathed in his boy smell, and looked upwards. *James, he's a cracker kid. Tell me how to do the right thing. Hell, tell me what the right thing is.*

'Where's Karina?' Mickey asked as he drove out

of town and onto the causeway heading to Nelson. On one side of the road were apple orchards, on the other a tidal estuary.

'At work.'

She enjoyed her job, and her enthusiasm for her busy life seemed endless, but could that be a cover for the hurt underneath? He'd begun to appreciate her need to make a haven from where she could look life in the eye.

'Why isn't she coming with us?'

'She's letting us have man-time together.' His nephew had latched on to Karina like a lifeline. *Well, duh, she* is *his lifeline. So get it sorted, get it right for her, make her life easier.*

His foot pressed harder on the accelerator. The lawyers were waiting.

The house was cold when Karina let herself in after work. The day had dragged, her body ached, and tears had regularly threatened but thankfully hadn't spilled. She couldn't have David or Leeann asking what was wrong, or the patients fussing over her.

In the lounge, she cursed. The fire hadn't been set. There was no kindling chopped, nor any wood in the basket. Those had become Logan's jobs over the time he'd been here, and obviously they hadn't been foremost in his mind when he was walking out.

Trudging outside to the woodshed, she picked up the hatchet and began splitting pine for kindling. Dinner. *Yeah, well, so what?* The chicken she'd planned on baking could stay in the fridge. About all she could face was toast. It wouldn't hurt Mickey this once.

'Let me do that. You're going to lose a finger unless you start watching what you're doing.'

She leapt up, dropping the axe at her feet. 'Don't creep up on me.'

Sadness leaked out of Logan's eyes. 'Let's not play those games. Mickey's inside, looking for you. I'll bring the wood in and be on my way.'

Gulp. He had a point. She had lashed out thoughtlessly.

'Thank you.'

'Karina, we went to Nelson.' Mickey's short arms wrapped around her thighs. 'It took a *long* time.'

Placing kisses on his head, she lifted him to

stare into his sweet face. 'You're home now.' She loved him so much it terrified her.

'Logan took me to a big building with lots of windows. The lady gave me a lemonade drink.'

'That was nice.' Where had Logan gone? To see his real estate agent? *Yeah, I bet he did. Of course he wants this house sold ASAP now that he's moved out.*

About to storm outside and give him a piece of her mind, she hesitated. *Slow down, think it through.* It wasn't as if he could sell without her signing papers for the trust lawyers. She'd wait and see what he said.

He said absolutely nothing about his jaunt over to the city.

'I've brought in enough kindling and wood for the rest of the week.'

Don't say a word. See if he'll talk about the house, or the surgery. Anything.

'Thank you.'

'See you tomorrow, Mickey.'

And he walked out.

That went well.

She snatched bread out of the pantry. A can of baked beans. Mickey's favourite dinner.

'I'm hungry.'

Right on cue.

'Set the table, then.'

He put three mats up, then three sets of cutlery. 'Where's Uncle Logan gone?'

That was the thing. She didn't know. Not that it was a problem. She had his phone number if she needed to get in touch.

'Into town, sweetheart.' *Please don't ask me anything else.*

'Will he be back to put me to bed?'

Did she want a tantrum? Or peace and quiet while they ate?

'Let's hope so.' Not quite a lie, but close enough to crank up the guilt.

Thankfully Mickey shrugged and dragged a stool over to the sink, filled three glasses with water. But when she tried to undress him for bed it was a different story.

'Where's Uncle Logan? I want him to read to me.'

'He's in town, sweetheart. Now, let's get your shirt off.'

'No.' He ducked out of reach.

Damn you, Logan Pascale. 'Mickey, come here.

Now.' She gritted her teeth and counted to ten. Stood up. 'Right. Get into bed. Clothes and all.'

She was done arguing.

'Why won't he help me?' Mickey bit his bottom lip and blinked as tears rolled down his face.

'He's busy.' She tentatively made to lift his shirt and was surprised when he let her. 'Where did you get those bruises?'

Her heart stilled as she studied the purple marks on his upper arm. Three dark marks about the size of a fifty cent piece. Too uniform for a bleeding disorder, surely?

Mickey shut his eyes. 'Don't know,' he whispered as he reached for his pyjama jacket to pull over his singlet.

'Did you bump into something at kindy, sweetheart?'

He nodded slowly and climbed into bed.

'You need to watch where you're going.'

After tucking him into bed, she read him stories until he fell asleep. Dropping a kiss on his forehead, she clicked off the light and headed to the lounge, curled up into a chair.

Where are you staying, Logan? In the firebox flames flicked against the glass, sending a warm glow over the tiles. *Will the motel proprietor look after you when the nightmare strikes?*

Tears spilled over and poured down to drip off her chin.

Can you bring back the pieces of my heart you've stolen? I can't let you keep them. This wasn't supposed to be so hard. *When did I fall for you? Was it that day I came home to find you lying in front of the fire, holding one tired little boy? Or the morning you brought me a cup of tea in bed because I'd got up to Mickey three times and to you once during the night?*

Could it have occurred during one of those nightmares, when anger and fear had glittered out of his grey eyes as he returned from that place of horror he went to in his sleep?

It didn't matter. It had happened. And she needed to do something about it. Pull up the barriers and protect what was left.

Her heart stuttered. *Too late*, her head screamed.

With an exasperated sigh she threw herself out of the chair and went to make hot chocolate. The heck with her hips. This was a serious situation and only chocolate would help. That or Logan apologising and then sitting down with her to talk through everything.

The spoon scraped against the bottom of the pot as she absently stirred the heating milk. Her hand shook slightly. How would she cope if the house was sold? Could she make a haven in another place? There'd been so many changes over the last few months. She wasn't ready for any more.

Suddenly she was afraid. Afraid of starting again, of finding that some of those things she'd strived to put behind her had come back to torment her.

Logan Pascale had already changed things by being—Logan. She'd been unsettled from the moment she'd first laid eyes on him. She'd begun to want, to wonder, to hope, to feel. There was more to life than what she had. She could have it all and survive happily. But only if she was prepared to step off the edge and give it a go.

There was the crux of the matter. She was not going to take a risk with her heart, her life, her everything ever again. It had been a lonely battle since Maria had died, but she couldn't let that rule her head. So, even loving Logan as she did, she had to keep him at arm's length. No, make that at the end of a rainbow. Unattainable. Out of temptation's way.

She had to ask him exactly what he was up to. His answer should dampen the fire in her belly.

Picking up the phone, she tapped Logan's number.

'Karina.'

'Do you like working in the clinic? Are you tempted to stay on permanently?'

Silence, then the sound of a chair being moved. 'That's why you've phoned?'

'Yes.'

Silence. Then, 'I can't.'

More silence.

She finally gave up waiting for him to expand on that. 'So you're determined to return to Africa?'

'Yes.'

That was all she got. *Yes*, with a load of caution behind it.

'Why?' She could also do short and to the point.

'It's where I work.'

'Oh, come on. You sign up for one contract at a time, not indefinitely.'

Dislike for herself rose and soured her mouth,

but she had a battle to fight and listening to her heart right now would not win what she needed from him.

Then Logan said, 'The doctors at your local hospital work from one contract to the next, too. That's how it's done. They still say they work in Nelson, or wherever.'

True.

'Aren't you worried you might get kidnapped again? Or worse?'

Her heart squeezed so tightly she feared she was having a cardiac incident. A medical one, not a romantic one. She did not want Logan facing danger again. He might not be quite so lucky next time.

'Of course I am—even when the odds are against it.'

She shut her eyes against the pain in his voice, against his courage and his need. Her chest rose and fell as deep, slow breaths filled her lungs, dribbled out. *I need to support him and let him go without laying on guilt for doing what he wants.*

So all she had to do was tell him to go, as she'd wanted to do all along, and yet something held her back. Her obstinate heart?

'I think I understand.'

'Do you? Really?'

His scepticism drove her to say, 'You're braver than me. By a long way.'

Hiss. The milk had boiled over. She swore. 'Sorry—got to go.' *Click.* End of conversation. *Wipe, wipe*—milk everywhere. Damn, damn—sob. Rinse, squeeze the cloth—sob, sob.

Tossing the cloth in the sink, she headed to bed for a long, sleepless night.

Somehow they had to work together in the morning. Could she pull a sick day? That would work. Not.

CHAPTER TWELVE

KARINA SURVIVED THE morning by avoiding
Logan as much as possible. Later she barely coped
when he returned Mickey to her at dinnertime,
and struggled with Mickey's tears and tantrums
when Logan walked out through the door to go
to his motel.

When Mickey refused to get undressed for bed
she knew with absolute certainty that she had to
walk away and let him have his way. She was in
danger of screaming at him. And she'd never for-
give herself if she let the despair that had dogged
her all day form into words to lash him with. None
of this was Mickey's fault.

'Go to bed in your clothes,' she said, and pulled
the covers down.

Mickey climbed into bed and turned his head
away.

'Goodnight, sweetheart.'

Silence was his answer. Had he been taking lessons from his uncle?

She cleaned up the kitchen, folded the washing, got some mince out of the freezer for tomorrow night's dinner, sat at the table with the mail, pushed that aside and got up. Turned off the lights and went to bed. Her body ached with tiredness. Her head was about to split in half. Her stomach was a knot.

She lay on her back, staring at the darkened ceiling, waiting for sleep to creep in and give her some relief from her thoughts for a while. Waited and waited.

'Karina…' Mickey stood by her bed. 'I'm lonely.'

You and me both, my boy.

She tossed the covers back. 'Come on, get in. We'll cuddle down together.'

She wrapped her arms around his body and held him close. And finally nodded off.

To dream of a hot, sexy man with demons in his head and concern for others in his heart…

'Wake up, Karina.' Mickey ran a finger over her eyelids.

Rolling over with a groan, she stared at the digital clock. Seven-thirty-five. What had happened? She never slept this late.

'Come on, sleepy head. Time we were up and about.' She pushed out of bed, feeling as if she'd done ten rounds with a heavyweight boxer. Except she'd never make the end of one bout. 'You have your shower first.'

'I don't want a shower.' Mickey still wore his clothes, and his flushed face was screwed up ready for an outburst.

'Okay, sweetheart, here's the deal. You can't go to see Uncle Logan if you don't shower.'

Since when had bribery become a part of her repertoire?

'I'll find you your favourite sweatshirt while you're getting clean.'

Blackmail as well?

He slid off the bed, thumping onto the floor. 'You can't come in the bathroom.'

Since when?

'Promise to wash your face, behind your ears and between your toes? And all parts in between?'

'Will Uncle Logan check?'

'Absolutely.'

Mickey dashed down to the bathroom, suddenly eager to get in the shower.

She could kill for a cup of tea and some headache pills. Not necessarily in that order.

She found Mickey's clothes for the day. Guilt at her handling of his reticence over showering bothered her. Using Logan as a bribe hadn't been right, but it had been the only thing to come to mind. Unfortunately the chances of Mickey forgetting by the time he saw his uncle were about zero. She'd deal with Logan's reaction when it happened.

She opened the bathroom door enough to slip the clothes through, then closed it and went to the kitchen to poke through the cupboard for painkillers.

'Where are they?'

Shifting recipe books, packets of antibiotics for Mickey's previous infections, she couldn't find what she wanted. They'd be in the bathroom cupboard.

'Go away!' Mickey shouted.

She'd completely forgotten she was banned from there. 'Sorry, Mickey, I'm going—'

His little torso was black and purple with bruising.

'Mickey? Sweetheart? What's happened?'

She knelt in front of him, took the towel out of his hands and began drying him ever so gently as she studied every part of him. Had she discovered the reason he hadn't wanted to undress for bed?

'I'm sorry.'

He was sorry?

'This isn't your fault, Mickey. You haven't done anything wrong.'

If he'd fallen he wouldn't have bruises on both his stomach and his chest, his back and his thighs. *Leukaemia.* The word landed in her brain like a bomb. Leukaemia. The dreaded disease that many children with Down syndrome contracted often first appeared as bruising due to low platelet numbers.

Leukaemia—with all its treatments and tests and transplants and—

I'm going to throw up.

Not in front of Mickey. Swallowing the bile, she struggled to get her stomach under control. Sweat broke out on her brow and upper lip.

'I haven't been naughty, Karina. Promise.' Fat tears ran down his face.

'I know you haven't,' she croaked, before dropping the towel and placing the softest kiss on each cheek. 'You're my man, and my man's good. Let's get you dressed and warm, then we'll call Uncle Logan.'

She wanted to hug him tight but didn't dare. What if she added to those bruises?

'Will he be angry at me?'

'No way. He loves you.' What was this about? 'Mickey, did someone hurt you?'

'No—o.'

Holding him carefully against her, she stood up. 'Let's get the phone.'

'I'm not going to hospital,' he hiccupped against her neck. 'I don't like being sick.'

'I know, sweetheart. I really do.' *Right now it's the last place I want to go too, but it's where we're headed.*

Logan answered on the first ring. 'Karina? You okay?'

'You need to come home and see Mickey. Urgently.'

'What's up?'

'He's covered in bruises. They're everywhere. What if it's AML?' The fear that had started in the bathroom bubbled up, almost overwhelming her. 'Logan!' she cried. 'He's so small, he doesn't need this.'

'Karina, stop it. You're panicking.'

Great for him to say when there was a tremor in his voice.

'There could be any number of reasons for the bruising. Not only acute myeloid leukaemia.'

Hearing him enunciate those dreaded words made her skin chill.

'The front and back of his body are covered.' She kissed the damp head nestled against her. 'He needs you.' *Damn it.* 'I need you.'

'Hang in there. I'll check him over, then if it's necessary we'll take him to hospital, get the specialists on to it immediately.'

Hurry up and get here. I need your strength. I can't do this on my own. Oh, no, Maria and James. Maria, I'm so sorry. Your baby's sick. I've let him down by not keeping him healthy.

Even though she knew perfectly well that no one could prevent leukaemia striking, the guilt was crawling through her frozen body.

I am so sorry.

'This is so hard, Logan. What if—?' She couldn't finish the sentence. Her throat was clogged with unshed tears.

'One thing at a time, okay? Unlock your door for me.'

'Mickey hid it from me.' She turned the lock to open. 'He refused to get undressed last night, slept in his clothes. Then he got into bed with me. I wasn't allowed to see him in the shower.'

Now she was blathering. Worse, she couldn't stop.

'If I hadn't gone in to get some pills I mightn't have known for another day. What sort of mother does that make me?'

'The best.'

A familiar hand touched her cheek in a caress, then removed the phone from her ear.

'The very best.'

Her eyes widened. 'That was quick.'

'I was walking out of my room the moment I heard your voice.' Logan turned his focus to Mickey. 'Hey, buddy, how's my boy?'

'I don't want to go to hospital, Uncle Logan.'

Logan raised an eyebrow in Karina's direction.

She shook her head. 'I never mentioned hospital.'

Logan held his arms out to Mickey. 'Can I hold you and get a hug, buddy?'

Mickey unwound his arms and reached towards Logan.

Logan held him as tenderly as he would the finest crystal. 'Let's go to the bathroom and you can show me your tummy.'

Karina held her breath, but the fight seemed to have gone out of Mickey. He cuddled close to his uncle and said nothing.

Karina didn't breathe again until Logan had done a short but thorough examination of Mickey's torso.

'These bruises could've been made by impact. With what? That is the question. But I'm not certain about anything. Best we go to Nelson ED and get some blood work done.'

'I'll get his jacket and shoes.' She had to get away from those trusting eyes Mickey had locked on her. 'I won't be a moment.'

She sat in the back of the car with Mickey in his car seat beside her. She couldn't take her eyes off him, as if she might be able to keep the baddies at bay if she didn't look away. His little hand gripped hers so tightly she'd probably never get the feeling back and she couldn't care less.

The trip took for ever, and yet they seemed to pull up in the hospital car park almost before they'd left Motueka. Logan carried him in to the ED and after a short conversation with the nurse on the reception desk they were shown through to Dr Cavanagh, a paediatrician.

Mickey started crying. 'I want to go home.'

'Shh, sweetheart. We're going to make you better.' *I'm not making promises I can't guarantee.* But, damn, she wanted to. Anything to take that misery away from his beloved face.

Karina took him from Logan and paced up and down, leaving the doctors to their discussion.

Then… 'Hello, Mickey. I'm Paddy—a doctor like your uncle. We're going to go into a little room so you can show me your tummy without everyone else seeing. Okay?'

His manner was so gentle Mickey didn't protest.

It didn't take long—as if Mickey had worked out that if he did what he was asked he'd get out of there quicker. Even when Paddy took some blood samples he only squeezed his eyes shut and turned his head into Karina's breast.

'Go get a coffee in the canteen. I'll be along the moment I know the answer to these.' Dr Cavanagh held up the blood tubes and a form.

'How do I sit here pretending my world isn't imploding?' she asked Logan ten minutes later, when he placed a mug of tea in front of her and put down a juice for Mickey.

It took for ever until Paddy strode through the canteen, a smile on his face. 'White cells, platelets and haemoglobin all normal—the rest will take longer. But we've ruled out the main players in AML.'

Tears of relief streamed down Karina's face, and when she glanced at Logan she saw pools of moisture in the corners of his eyes. Taking his free hand in hers she stood. 'Come on, Mickey, we're taking you home.'

Paddy cleared his throat. 'Actually, as we still don't know what caused those bruises, I need you to stick around a bit longer. In cases like this there are certain procedures I need to follow. Mickey, is it okay if I ask you a few questions?'

Mickey nodded and gripped Karina's hand.

'Mickey, has anyone been hurting you?' Paddy asked him gently.

Logan looked shocked. 'Are you suggesting he's being pushed around at home?'

Karina felt the bottom fall out of her world when only seconds ago she'd started to feel relief and hope. Did the doctor think that she'd been hurting Mickey?

'It's okay, Mickey,' she whispered, feeling sick to her stomach. 'You can tell the truth. Has anyone been hurting you?'

Slowly, Mickey nodded again. 'Ben.'

Ben? Suddenly her conversation with Robyn flooded back to her.

'Is Ben the new boy in your class?'

Mickey sniffed. 'He says I look funny. If I try to play with him and William, Ben pinches me and tells me to go away.'

All the arguments about his not wanting to go to kindy came back. 'I thought Mickey was being clingy and wanting to hang around with Logan when he refused to go to kindy.'

She looked to Logan, saw anger and compassion warring for supremacy in his eyes. Not anger ather, surely? Yes, she'd made a mistake, but—

He tucked an arm over her shoulders. 'We've been worrying too much about the medical and not enough about the human factor.'

Phew. She relaxed against him. 'Why would a kid do that to a sweet wee boy who never hurts anyone?'

Paddy intervened. 'You'd be shocked at how much of that I see in here. Now, go home, take some time to make your lad feel safe and secure about the world out there, and give yourselves a break. It's a rare parent who looks for bullying straight away. I'll call you as soon as I have those other results.'

So they weren't out of the woods yet. Karina smiled her thanks for this man who'd dropped everything to see Mickey, even when he was obviously asleep on his feet after a night shift.

Logan shook his hand and took her elbow. 'Let's go. What do you reckon, Mickey? Want to see Mr Grumpy?'

'Do I look like an idiot, Uncle Logan?'

Karina's heart froze. 'No, you don't,' she growled, then softened her tone. 'No, you are not an idiot, Mickey. You're the best little boy in the world.'

'You're awesome, buddy.' Logan's arms came

around them both, held them as he breathed through the anger tensing his body. 'And I thought what happened to me in Nigeria was bad,' he whispered against her ear.

Back home, they left Mickey with Mr Grumpy, after he'd eaten baked beans on toast for a late breakfast, and headed out to see his kindergarten teachers. Paddy had called to tell them the other tests were normal.

'You were right. I worry too much about the wrong things. I should've listened harder to Mickey.'

Logan took her hand as they walked up the path to the kindergarten. 'Blaming yourself is a waste of time. You're a great mother to him. Just keep believing that.'

The teachers were shocked, but admitted that they had noticed changes in Mickey's attitude and how lately he'd often avoided going out to play at break time. They hadn't made the connection between Mickey's behaviour and Ben joining the class, but when William and the other children were questioned they admitted that they had seen Ben hurting Mickey.

The teachers assured Karina and Logan that they'd speak to Ben's parents and it wouldn't happen again.

'How could they not have noticed?' Karina snapped as she buckled her seatbelt for the short ride home. 'We'll take Mickey out of here and enrol him in another kindergarten.'

Logan shook his head slowly. 'I don't know... This'll happen again wherever he goes. He's different, and kids always pick up on that.'

Feeling let down, she rounded on him, only to have him hold his hand up.

'Hear me out. He needs to learn to stand up for himself—not to run and hide.'

'Sure, Logan, and how's he going to do that?'

'I'll be there for him; with him. I'm going to kindy every day until he feels comfortable, and then I'm going to keep talking to him about what happened so he never again thinks he has to hide anything from us.'

Huh? 'What are you talking about? You're leaving in a week.'

'I'm staying. Permanently.'

Logan hadn't thought it through, but the moment the words left his mouth he knew it was true. Here in Motueka, with Karina and Mickey, he'd found what he'd been looking for most of his adult life.

A hand pushed at his shoulder.

'Stop it. You can't go from selling the house and the surgery and bailing out to suddenly telling me you're staying. Do you ever consult with other people before you make decisions that might affect them?'

She was peeved.

'I'm not selling the house or the surgery. I sorted it all with the lawyers yesterday, in Nelson.'

'That's not answering my question.'

She locked her eyes on him and waited, her fingers tugging at the hem of her jacket.

He'd done what she wanted, hadn't he? What was there to discuss?

'Is it all right with you if I'm a permanent fixture in my nephew's life?'

Disappointment replaced her annoyance. 'You know it is. What's not all right is the way you go about doing things that involve me. I've spent my life falling into line to suit first my father and then Ian. I am *not* going to do it for you. Ever.'

So she thought he was a control freak? 'I was trying to do the best for you both.'

'Take me home. I'm done here.' She turned to face the front, her shoulders tight, her hands still fidgeting. 'I'm done with you.'

His heart curled up tight, painfully. Until she'd said that he hadn't realised how much he'd been hoping she cared for him.

'I'm still not going away.'

'Mickey will be thrilled.'

Did Karina want him gone so she could bring Mickey up on her own? He doubted it. She'd phoned him the moment she found those bruises, had turned to him for help. She was tough on the outside, but underneath was a softie who sometimes needed to be able to lean on someone. *Him.* He had to be her backstop. He couldn't handle it if she found someone else to fill that gap in her life.

Could he win her heart in the months ahead? It wouldn't be easy, but the reward would be worth all the waiting.

Karina stood in the doorway of what had briefly been Logan's bedroom. Her heart thudded against her ribs. Tears blocked her throat. Logan sat on the floor with Mickey kneeling beside him. In front of them was an open carton of James's belongings.

Photos covered the carpet, many of them torn or crinkled from being screwed up. The photo of James in Logan's hand was shaking.

'That's my daddy.' Mickey tapped the picture. He rummaged through the others. 'And here's Mummy. She's pretty.'

'Yes, buddy, she is.' Logan's voice sounded full of tears. He was focused on the picture of his brother, drinking in every pixel.

'I want them to come home now.' Mickey picked up some more photos.

Logan ran a hand over Mickey's head and down his back. 'You and me both, buddy.'

Tears spilled down Karina's cheeks. 'And me,' she whispered.

'Hey.' Logan looked up. 'We're doing a bit of sorting here.'

'Sure.' She took a step into the room. 'I had to put the photos away. They got too much for a certain boy. He wasn't coping.'

'Hence the damaged ones?'

She nodded. 'That's why there's only the one on the wall in his bedroom.' Out of reach of Mickey.

'Karina, can I put Mummy and Daddy in my bedroom now?'

'Yes, sweetheart, you can.'

Hopefully enough time had passed that he would no longer get too distraught every time he looked at the photos. She moved closer and squatted down beside Mickey.

'You choose which ones you'd like.'

'Uncle Logan's staying with us.'

Her gaze instantly fixed on Logan. As in staying in this house? Or in Motueka? 'You've explained?'

'Of course. But I didn't say exactly where I'd be living.' His eyes never wavered. 'I can find a house close by.'

'Or you could move in with us.'

How would she cope? How could she not? She loved him. Loved *them*. They were a family unit, put together under unusual circumstances, but that didn't mean the love wasn't real or strong or good.

I love them both so much it hurts.

She loved Mickey; always had and always would. She loved Logan: always would. She'd done what she'd sworn never to do again: fallen in love. Fallen for Logan. Surprisingly, that didn't feel like a problem right now. He might act first, tell her later, but he always had her concerns on his radar, looking out for her and Mickey.

Was she going to ruin a chance at happiness by being pig-headed? He hadn't brushed her aside when she'd complained he should have discussed everything with her. He'd been at the front door as fast as possible when she'd phoned in a panic that morning. What more did she want?

For Logan to love her.

She stared at him. Would he ever feel for her what was tightening her chest, speeding up her heart for him? Did he get tingles at the base of his spine every time she walked into the same room? Tingles she'd come to accept as her Logan barometer?

Only one way to find out all the answers.

The air was suddenly chilly, but her blood was warm, her heart heated. 'Hey…' She leaned across and took his face in her hands, kissed him full on the mouth.

'Tell me I'm not dreaming,' the man holding her heart whispered.

Her reply was to kiss him some more.

'I could get to like this.'

Now he took charge of the kiss, deepening it and sending hot need flowing through her body.

Finally she pulled her head back, just enough to see into his eyes. 'I know I'm all over the place about what I want, but I'd be happy if you stayed here. Permanently. With us. For Mickey. For me. I love you, which is why I got huffy with you. I didn't think I could take a chance on happiness, but now I know I can't do anything else. You've found a way into my heart. Not sure how, but you have.'

Her lips pressed together in a rueful smile. She could go on and on, but he'd probably do a runner from the madwoman.

Logan reached a hand around one of hers. 'I'm not going back to Africa. After this morning I know I don't need to. I have you. Nothing, no one, is half as scary with you at my side.'

'Kar—ina. You want a photo?'

'Sure do, sweetheart. You pick one for me.'

She slowly slipped out of Logan's hold, unwilling to leave his warmth and strength, but knowing those would always be there for her, whenever she wanted them. She just knew it.

'Karina...' He pulled her back to him. 'I love you, too. You're amazing, the way you've accepted who I am, the mess I've been. I doubt I'd have begun to recover without you there for me. But most of all I just love you—everything about you.'

Her heart swelled and more tears flowed—this time for joy.

'Thank you,' she croaked.

This time she'd got it right. She knew it from the bottom of her heart.

Logan stared down at a picture of his brother and sister-in-law. 'I wonder what those two would have to say about this.'

'I think Maria would be laughing fit to bust. In the nicest possible way, of course.'

'James would tell me to grab life and live it with you and Mickey.'

One month later...

A handful of people were gathered in the lounge at the old house in High Street. Karina looked around, smiling at everyone.

Mickey's grandparents, Adele and Mark, were smiling nearly as much as she was. David and his wife and Leeann and her partner were chatting together. David was more relaxed now that he could share the clinic's workload with Logan, and no longer talked of moving away. Becca stood in the middle of the room, watching everyone as if she was the boss around here. All dressed up in a figure-hugging suit, looking stunning, she had a new boyfriend at her side who looked as though he never intended letting her get away. Jonty, dressed in his Sunday best, stood with an excited Mickey.

This was what life was all about—what she'd been searching for most of her life. Warmth and happiness.

'I'm sorry your parents couldn't be here.' Logan spoke quietly to Karina as they waited for Becca to start the proceedings.

So am I.

'Don't be. It's their loss, not ours.' Karina refused to let her mum and dad hurt her again, especially today of all days.

She had Adele and Mark now. They made her feel welcome and loved, with no pressure about how she did things—including raising their grandson—with the kind of family love she wanted and revelled in. But it was only a drop in the bucket of love she received from Logan every minute of every day.

She glanced down at the simple cream silk dress she wore and knew nothing but happiness. It was a beautiful outfit. One she'd wear again and again when she and Logan went out for an intimate meal. Her life had been turned around.

Becca approached with a huge I-told-you-so smile. 'Ready?'

Karina laughed. 'I've been ready for weeks.'

'Then let's do it.' Logan took her free hand and locked those beautiful grey eyes on her.

Becca turned to face their guests. 'I know the marriage celebrant isn't supposed to cry, but this is my first wedding, and Karina is my best friend, so you'll have to put up with a few tears as we go through the ceremony.'

Jonty grumped, 'Get on with it, girl. Lunch is spoiling.'

Karina's heart squeezed. Here it was. The moment she joined her life with the best man ever. A man who'd always look out for her and Mickey, who wouldn't deliberately break her heart or trash her love. A man she'd give her life for, who would share raising Mickey, would cherish for ever.

In one hand she gripped Logan's fingers tightly. In the other she held a bunch of the first of the season's daffodils, grown and picked for her by Jonty. The spring flowers spoke of new beginnings and brighter days to come.

Leaning close to Logan, she whispered, 'I love you.'

'I know,' he whispered back, with a cheeky glint in those eyes she adored.

Eyes that expressed so much of who Logan was. She'd seen pain and fear in them, anger and stubbornness. She'd also read love and wonder and care and concern for her and for Mickey. Those eyes had led her to this moment.

'Becca, we're ready,' she said around a big smile. She was done waiting. 'Do it.'

She mightn't be concerned about lunch, but she sure was bursting to become Karina Pascale.

Mickey stood beside Becca, his cute little face so serious it must be hurting him.

'I've got the ring in my pocket, Uncle Logan.'

Maria, you'd be so proud of your wee man. He

looks gorgeous. He's growing up fast, and he's absolutely devoted to Logan. I wish you could see him right this minute, standing proud and tall for us.

Tears ran down Karina's cheeks. 'And we haven't even started!'

Becca took the hint, cleared her throat and began.

'Love. That's what brought Karina and Logan together. First their love for Mickey, then their love for each other.' She swallowed hard. 'The day Karina said she had to get home to her men I knew she was a goner.'

The room was quiet, as though the few guests were holding their breath for fear of missing a single word.

'These three people have a very special relationship. Today I'm marrying Karina, Logan *and* Mickey. They will look out for each other in the good times and the bad times; they'll always be there for each other. Their love will conquer everything as it's already shown us.'

Becca turned to Karina, tears glistening in the corners of her eyes.

'Karina Brown, will you take this man to be your lawful wedded husband?'

Her throat ached, her eyes moistened as she looked into Logan's eyes, but her voice came through loud and clear. 'Yes, I will.'

'Logan Pascale, will you take this woman to be your lawful wedded wife, and look after her every minute for the rest of your life?'

Karina grinned. Her friend was nailing him. She winked at her man.

His fingers squeezed hers. 'Yes, to both questions.'

'Mickey, can you pass Uncle Logan the ring please?'

Mickey solemnly placed the ring in Logan's hand.

Karina's hand shook as Logan slid the band of gold on to her finger.

'I love you, Karina, more than life itself.'

Becca nodded. 'I declare you married. Logan, feel free to kiss your wife.'

'Like I need telling twice.' He leaned close. 'Love you, Mrs Pascale.'

Then his mouth claimed hers amidst cheers

from their family and friends, who were raising glasses of champagne in their direction.

Of course Mr Grumpy had the last word.

'Now we can eat.'

* * * * *

MILLS & BOON®
Large Print Medical

October

JUST ONE NIGHT?	Carol Marinelli
MEANT-TO-BE FAMILY	Marion Lennox
THE SOLDIER SHE COULD NEVER FORGET	Tina Beckett
THE DOCTOR'S REDEMPTION	Susan Carlisle
WANTED: PARENTS FOR A BABY!	Laura Iding
HIS PERFECT BRIDE?	Louisa Heaton

November

ALWAYS THE MIDWIFE	Alison Roberts
MIDWIFE'S BABY BUMP	Susanne Hampton
A KISS TO MELT HER HEART	Emily Forbes
TEMPTED BY HER ITALIAN SURGEON	Louisa George
DARING TO DATE HER EX	Annie Claydon
THE ONE MAN TO HEAL HER	Meredith Webber

December

MIDWIFE...TO MUM!	Sue MacKay
HIS BEST FRIEND'S BABY	Susan Carlisle
ITALIAN SURGEON TO THE STARS	Melanie Milburne
HER GREEK DOCTOR'S PROPOSAL	Robin Gianna
NEW YORK DOC TO BLUSHING BRIDE	Janice Lynn
STILL MARRIED TO HER EX!	Lucy Clark